**P9-CQD-616**

## Nash groaned as heat and pressure poured into him.

It was bad enough he'd had a restless night filled with erotic dreams of his hostess. But there, wearing jeans and a T-shirt, Stephanie stood in the doorway, a piece of sandpaper in each hand. Nash watched as she reached up and rubbed at a spot well above her head. Her T-shirt rode up, exposing a bit of stomach. What was it about this woman and her belly?

"You need a ladder," he said, surprising her.

Stephanie jumped and squeaked, then glared at him. "I swear I'm going to buy you a collar with a bell and make you wear it."

"You'll have to wrestle me into submission first."

He'd meant the comment as a joke, but at his words, her eyes darkened and awareness sharpened her features. Tension crackled in the empty room.

So his attraction wasn't all one-sided, he thought with satisfaction.

Dear Reader,

Welcome to more juicy reads from Silhouette Special Edition. I'd like to highlight Silhouette veteran and RITA® Award finalist Teresa Hill, who has written over ten Silhouette books under the pseudonym Sally Tyler Hayes. Her second story for us, *Heard It Through the Grapevine,* has all the ingredients for a fast-paced read—marriage of convenience, a pregnant preacher's daughter and a handsome hero to save the day. Teresa Hill writes, "I love this heroine because she takes a tremendous leap of faith. She hopes that her love will break down the hero's walls, and she never holds back." Don't miss this touching story!

*USA TODAY* bestselling and award-winning author Susan Mallery returns to her popular miniseries HOMETOWN HEARTBREAKERS with *One in a Million.* Here, a sassy single mom falls for a drop-dead-gorgeous FBI agent, but sets a few ground rules—a little romance, no strings attached. Of course, we know rules are meant to be broken! Victoria Pade delights us with *The Baby Surprise,* the last in her BABY TIMES THREE miniseries, in which a confirmed bachelor discovers he may be a father. With encouragement from a beautiful heroine, he feels ready to be a parent…and a husband.

The next book in Laurie Paige's SEVEN DEVILS miniseries, *The One and Only* features a desirable medical assistant with a secret past who snags the attention of a very charming doctor. Judith Lyons brings us *Alaskan Nights,* which involves two opposites who find each other irritating, yet totally irresistible! Can these two survive a little engine trouble in the wilderness? In *A Mother's Secret,* Pat Warren tells of a mother in search of her secret child and the discovery of the man of her dreams.

This month is all about love against the odds and finding that special someone when you least expect it. As you lounge in your favorite chair, lose yourself in one of these gems!

Sincerely,

Karen Taylor Richman
Senior Editor

Please address questions and book requests to:
Silhouette Reader Service
U.S.: 3010 Walden Ave., P.O. Box 1325, Buffalo, NY 14269
Canadian: P.O. Box 609, Fort Erie, Ont. L2A 5X3

# Susan Mallery

## ONE IN A MILLION

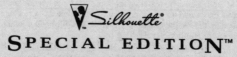

Silhouette®

# SPECIAL EDITION™

Published by Silhouette Books

**America's Publisher of Contemporary Romance**

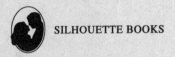 SILHOUETTE BOOKS

ISBN 0-373-24543-2

ONE IN A MILLION

Copyright © 2003 by Susan Macias Redmond

Visit Silhouette at www.eHarlequin.com

**Printed in U.S.A.**

# SUSAN MALLERY

is the bestselling and award-winning author of over fifty books for Harlequin and Silhouette Books. She makes her home in the Pacific Northwest with her handsome prince of a husband and her two adorable-but-not-bright cats.

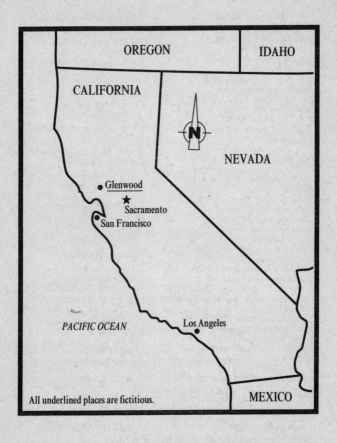

All underlined places are fictitious.

## Chapter One

Good-looking men should not be allowed to show up on one's doorstep without at least twenty-four hours' notice, Stephanie Wynne thought wearily as she leaned against her front door and tried not to think about the fact that she hadn't slept in nearly forty-eight hours, couldn't remember her last shower and knew that her short, blond hair looked as if it had been cut with a rice thresher.

Three kids down with stomach flu had a way of taking the sparkle and glamour out of a woman's day. Not that the man in front of her was going to care about her personal problems.

Despite the fact that it was nearly two in the morning, the handsome, well-dressed stranger standing on her porch looked rested, tidy and really tall. She glanced from his elegant suit to the stained and torn football jersey she'd pulled out of the rag bag when she'd run out of clean clothes about two days ago because…

Her tired brain struggled for the reason.

Oh, yeah. The washer was broken.

Again, not something he was going to sweat about. Paying guests only wanted excellent service, quiet rooms and calorie-laden breakfasts.

She did her best to forget her pathetic appearance and forced her mouth into what she hoped was a friendly smile.

"You must be Nash Harmon. Thanks for calling earlier and letting me know you'd be arriving late."

"My flight out of Chicago was delayed." He drew his dark eyebrows together as he looked her up and down. "I hope I didn't wake you, Mrs.…"

"Wynne. Stephanie Wynne." She stepped back into the foyer of the old Victorian house. "Welcome to Serenity House."

The awful name for the bed and breakfast had been her late husband's idea. After three years she could speak it without wincing, but only just. If not for the very expensive custom-made stained-glass sign that had replaced a front window and the fact that her kids would object, Stephanie would have changed the name of the B&B in a heartbeat.

Her guest carried a leather duffle and a garment bag into the house. Her gaze moved between his expensive leather boots and her own mouse slippers with their tattered ears. When she finally headed upstairs to her own bed, she must remember *not* to look at herself in the mirror. Confirming her worst fears would cause her to shriek and wake the boys.

The man signed the registration card she'd left on the front desk and she took an imprint of his credit card. Once she'd received approval, she handed him an old-fashioned brass key.

"Your room is this way," she said, heading up the stairs.

She'd put him in the front bedroom. Not only was it large and comfortable, with a view of Glenwood, but it was one of only two guest rooms that weren't under her third-floor apartment. When she wasn't completely booked, she found it much easier to have guests stay there than to constantly keep at her kids to stay quiet. Being loud and being a boy seemed to go hand-in-hand.

Five minutes later she'd explained the amenities of the room, said she would be serving breakfast from seven-thirty to nine and asked him if he would like her to leave a newspaper outside his door in the morning.

He refused the paper.

She nodded and headed for the hallway.

"Mrs. Wynne?"

She turned back to look at him. "Stephanie, please."

He nodded. "Do you have a map of the area? I'm here to visit some people and I don't know my way around."

"Sure. Downstairs. I'll put one out for you at breakfast."

"Thank you."

He offered her a slight smile, one that didn't touch his eyes. It was late and she was so tired that her eyelashes hurt. But instead of leaving that second, she hesitated. Oh, not more than a heartbeat, but just long enough to notice that the overhead light brought out brownish highlights in his close-cropped black hair and that the hint of dark stubble on his square jaw made him look just a little bit dangerous.

Yeah, right, Stephanie thought as she turned away. Apparently she'd moved into the hallucination stage of sleep deprivation. Dangerous men didn't come to places like Glenwood. No doubt Nash Harmon was something completely harmless like a shoe salesman or a professor. Besides, what he did for a living was none of her business. As long as his credit-card company put the right amount of money into her bank account, she didn't care if her guest was a computer programmer or a pirate.

As for him being somewhat good-looking and possibly single—there hadn't been a wedding ring on his left hand—she couldn't care less. While her friends occasionally got on her case for not being willing to jump back into the man-infested dating pool, Stephanie ignored their well-meant intentions. She'd already been married once, thank you very much. Nine years as Marty's wife had taught her that while Marty looked like a grown-up on the outside, he'd been as irresponsible and self-absorbed as any ten-year-old on the inside. She would have gotten more cooperation and teamwork from a dog.

Marty had cured her of ever wanting another man around. While on occasion she would admit to getting lonely, and yes, the sex was tough to live without, it beat the alternative. She already had three kids to worry about. Getting involved with a man would be like adding a fourth child to the mix. She didn't think her nerves could stand it.

Despite his late night, Nash woke shortly after six the following morning. He glanced at the clock and compared it to his watch, which was still on Central Time. Then he rolled onto his back and stared at the ivory ceiling.

What the hell was he doing here?

Dumb question, he told himself. He already knew the answer. He was in a town he'd never heard of until a couple of weeks ago, to meet family he hadn't known he had. No. That wasn't completely true. He was in town because he'd been forced to take some vacation and he hadn't had anywhere else to go. If he'd tried laying low in Chicago, Kevin, his twin and already camped out at Glenwood, would have been on the next plane east.

Nash sat up and pushed back the covers. Without the routine of work, his day stretched endlessly in front of him. Had he really gotten so lost in the job that he didn't have anything else in his life?

Dumb question number two.

He knew he was going to have to get in touch with Kevin sometime that morning and set up a meeting. After thirty-one years of knowing nothing about their biological father save the fact that he'd gotten a seventeen-year-old virgin pregnant with twins and then abandoned her, he and Kevin were about to meet up with half siblings they'd never known they had.

Kevin thought finding out about more family was a good thing. Nash still needed convincing.

By 6:40 he'd showered, shaved and dressed in jeans, a long-sleeved shirt and boots. While it was mid-June, a cool fog hung over the part of the town he could see from his second-story window. Nash paced restlessly in his comfortable room. Maybe he would tell his hostess to forget about breakfast. He could go for a drive and eat at a diner somewhere. Or maybe he'd just keep going until he figured out why, in the past few months, he'd stopped sleeping, stopped eating, stopped giving a damn about anything but his job.

He grabbed the keys for his rental car, then headed downstairs. At the front desk, he tore off a sheet of notepaper and a pen, then paused when he heard noises from the rear of the house. If the owner was up, he could simply tell her he was skipping breakfast in person.

He followed the noise down a long hallway and through a set of closed swinging doors. When he stepped into the brightly lit kitchen, he was instantly assaulted by the scents of something baking and fresh coffee. His mouth watered and his stomach growled.

He glanced around, but the big, white-on-white kitchen was empty. A tray sat on a center island. A coffee carafe stood by an empty cup and saucer. Plastic wrap covered a plate of fresh fruit. By the stove, an open box of eggs waited beside a frying pan. Through a door on his left, he heard mumbled conversation.

He started toward the female voice and crossed the threshold. A woman stood on tiptoe in front of shelves. As he watched, she reached up for something on the top shelf, but her fingers only grazed the edge of the shelf.

Nash stepped forward to offer help, but at that moment the woman reached a little higher. Her cropped sweater rose above the waistband of her black slacks, exposing a sliver of bare skin.

Nash felt as if he'd been hit upside the head with

a two-by-four. His vision narrowed, sound faded and by gosh, he found himself experiencing the first flicker of life below his waist that he'd felt in damn near two years.

Over an inch of belly? He was in a whole lot more trouble than he'd realized. Apparently his boss had been right about him burning out.

A loud shriek brought him back to the here and now. Nash moved his gaze from the woman's midsection to her face and saw his hostess staring at him with wide eyes. She pressed a hand to her chest and sucked in a breath.

"You nearly scared the life out of me, Mr. Harmon. I didn't realize you were up already."

"Call me Nash," he said as he stepped forward and reached up for the top shelf. "What do you need?"

"That blue bag. There's a silver bread basket inside. I'm making scones and I usually put them in the larger basket but as you're my only guest at present, I thought something smaller would work."

He grasped the blue bag and felt something hard inside. After lowering it, he handed it to her. She took it with a shake of her head.

"I always meant to be tall," she told him. "Somehow I never got around to it."

"I wasn't aware it wasn't something you could get around to. I thought it just happened."

"Or not." She unzipped the bag and pulled out a silver wire basket. "Thanks for the help. Would you like some coffee?"

"Sure."

He led the way back into the kitchen. While he leaned against the counter, she ran hot water into the carafe, then drained it and wiped it dry. After filling it with coffee, she turned back to him.

"Cream and sugar?"

"Just black."

"The scones should be ready in about five minutes. I had planned to make you an omelette this morning. Ham? Cheese? Mushrooms?"

Last night he'd barely noticed her. What he remembered had been someone female, tired and strangely dressed. He had a vague recollection of spiky blond hair. Now he saw that Stephanie Wynne was a petite blonde with wide blue eyes and a full mouth that turned up at the corners. She wore her short hair in a sleek style that left her ears and neck bare. Tailored black slacks and a slightly snug sweater showed him that despite the small package, everything was where it needed to be. She was pretty.

And he'd noticed.

Nash tried to figure out the last time he'd noticed a woman—any woman—enough to classify her as pretty, ugly or something in between. Not for two years, he decided, knowing that figuring out the date hadn't been much of a stretch.

"Don't bother with eggs," he said. "Coffee and the scones are fine." He glanced at the tray. "And the fruit."

Stephanie frowned. "The room comes with a full breakfast. Aren't you hungry?"

More than he'd been in a while, but less than he should have been. "Maybe tomorrow," he said instead.

A timer on the stove beeped softly. Stephanie picked up two mitts and pulled open the oven door.

The scent of baked goods got stronger. Nash inhaled the fragrance of orange and lemon.

When she'd set two cookie sheets of scones onto cooling racks, she dug through a drawer and pulled out a linen napkin, then draped it in the silver basket.

"This morning we have orange, lemon and white chocolate scones," she said as she pulled a small crystal dish of butter from the refrigerator. "They're all delicious, which is probably tacky of me to say seeing as I made them, but it's true. Being a man, you won't care about the calories, so that's a plus."

She offered him a smile that made the corners of her eyes crinkle, then nodded toward the door next to him.

"The dining room is through there."

He took the hint and moved through to the next room. He found a large table set for one. The local paper lay on top of a copy of *USA TODAY*.

Stephanie followed him into the room, but waited until he was seated before serving him his breakfast. She poured coffee, removed the plastic wrap from his plate of fruit and made sure the butter was within easy reach. Then she wished him *"bon appétit"* before disappearing back into the kitchen.

Nash picked up one of the still-steaming scones. The scent of orange drifted to him. His stomach still growling, he took a bite.

Delicate flavors melted on his tongue. Hunger roared through him, as unfamiliar as it was welcome. He sipped the coffee next, then tried a strawberry. Everything tasted delicious. He couldn't remember the last meal he'd enjoyed, nor did he care. Instead he plowed through four scones, all the fruit and the entire carafe of coffee. When he was finally full, he pulled the copy of *USA TODAY* toward him and started to read.

A burst of laughter interrupted his perusal of the business section. He frowned as he realized he'd been hearing more than just Stephanie in the kitchen for some time. The other voices were low and difficult to make out. A husband? Probably.

The thought of a Mr. Wynne caused Nash a twinge of guilt. He didn't usually go around looking at other men's wives and admiring their bare skin.

He turned the page on the paper and started to read again, only to be interrupted by the sound of footsteps racing down the hall. He looked up in time to see three boys running toward the front door.

"Walk! We have a guest."

The command came from the kitchen. Instantly three pairs of feet slowed and three heads turned in his direction. Nash had a brief impression of towheaded boys ranging in age from ten or twelve to about eight. The two youngest were twins.

Stephanie stepped into view and gave him an apologetic smile. "Sorry. It's the last week of school and they're pretty wound up."

"No problem."

The boys continued to study him curiously until their mother shooed them out the door. The twins ducked back in for a quick kiss, then waved in his direction and disappeared. Stephanie stood in the foyer with the door open until a bus pulled up in front of the house. Through the window in the dining room Nash could see the boys climb onto the bus. When it pulled away, Stephanie closed the front door and walked into the dining room.

"Did you get enough to eat?" she asked as she began to clear his dishes. "There are more scones."

"I'm fine," he told her. "Everything was great."

"Thank you. The original scone recipe dates back several generations. My late husband and I rented a guest house from an English couple many years ago. Mrs. Frobisher was a great one for baking. She taught me how to make the scones. I also make shortbread cookies that melt in your mouth. I would be happy to leave a few in your room if you'd like."

Nash told himself that her mention of a "late husband" didn't mean much more than that he didn't have to feel guilty for noticing Stephanie's bare stomach. The entire point of their encounter earlier that morning was that he wasn't as dead inside as he'd thought. Good news that was not particularly meaningful.

He glanced at her face and saw the expectant expression in her blue eyes. His brain offered a replay of her conversation and he cleared his throat.

"If it's not too much trouble," he said.

"None at all. The boys prefer chocolate chip cookies. I guess shortbread is an acquired taste that comes with age."

She offered a polite smile and carried his dishes out of the dining room.

Nash flipped through the sports section, then closed the paper. The news no longer interested him. Maybe he would go for that drive now and explore the area.

He rose, then paused, not sure if he should tell his hostess he was leaving. When he traveled it was usually on business and he always stayed in anonymous hotels and motels. He'd never been in a bed and breakfast before. While this was a place of business, apparently it was also Stephanie's home.

He looked from the kitchen to the foyer, then decided she wouldn't care what he had planned for his day. After fishing his car keys out of his pocket, he walked across the gleaming hardwood floor and out to the curb where he'd left his rental car.

Two minutes later he was back in the Victorian house. He walked into the kitchen, but it was empty. He crossed to the stairs and glanced up. Was she cleaning his room, or had she gone up to her private quarters?

A loud bang made him turn toward the back of the house. He followed the rhythmic noise past the kitchen and pantry into a large utility room. Stephanie sat on the floor in front of a washer. An open manual lay on her lap and there were tools and assorted parts all around her.

In the ten or fifteen minutes since she'd cleared his table, she'd changed her clothes. The tailored slacks and attractive sweater had been replaced by worn jeans and a sweatshirt featuring a familiar cartoon mouse. As he watched, she jabbed the side of the washer with a large wrench.

"Rat-fink cheap piece of metal trash," she muttered. "I hate you. I will always hate you. For the rest of your life, you're going to have to live with that."

He cleared his throat.

Stephanie gasped and shifted on the floor so that she faced him. Her eyes widened and her mouth twisted into a half smile that was as much sheepish as amused.

"If you keep sneaking up on me like this, I'm going to be forced to put a bell around your neck."

Nash leaned against the door frame and nodded at the washer. "Is there a problem?"

"It's not working. I'm trying to use guilt, but I don't think it's helping." She glanced from him to her jeans and back. "I thought you were heading out."

"The battery in my rental car is dead."

"Did you try guilting it into behaving?"

"I thought a jump would be more effective."

"Sure."

She tossed down the wrench and rose. Wearing athletic shoes, she barely came to his shoulder. She gave the washer one more kick, then walked toward him.

"Lead the way."

Nash straightened. "I could take a look at that if you would like."

Stephanie appeared doubtful. "You don't strike me as the washer repairman type."

"I'm not, but I'm pretty mechanical."

"Thanks, but I'm going to get a professional in. I'll go get my car keys. Why don't you meet me in front?"

Stephanie waited until Nash had started down the hallway before running upstairs to get the keys out of her purse. When she reached the top floor, she told herself that her rapidly beating heart had everything to do with the effort required to climb two flights of stairs and nothing to do with her guest's appearance. She figured she was being about sixty percent honest.

The truth was Mr. Elegant-in-a-Suit looked just

as good in jeans as he had all dressed up. Daylight suited him, as well. Despite the fact that he couldn't have gotten more than four hours of sleep, he looked tanned, handsome and rested. She, of course, had dark circles that had defied her heavy-duty concealer and a bone-deep weariness compounded by a broken washer and an as-ever challenged bank account.

She took the back stairs down to the rear entrance and climbed into her minivan. After backing out of the driveway, she positioned her car so her bumper nearly touched his.

Jumper cables proved to be something of a challenge, but after rooting around in the garage for a few minutes, she found a set behind a box of old spare parts for some mystery machine. She picked them up and turned, only to run smack into Nash.

"You all right?" he asked as he grabbed her upper arms to steady her.

All right? With her nose practically touching his chest and her hands thrust into his rock-hard stomach?

He smelled good, she thought wistfully as she inhaled the scent of soap and man. Something deep inside her, that feminine part of her dormant for the past three years, gave a slight hiccup of resurrection and slowly stirred to life. Awareness rippled through her. Awareness and sexual interest.

Telling herself that the good news was that this would be a great story to tell her friends the next time they managed to sneak away for a girls'-only dinner, she stepped back and cleared her throat.

"Okay. While I'm out today I'm definitely getting you that bell." She handed him the jumper cables. "Hooking them up is going to be your problem. I know what a car battery looks like, but if I used those things, I would probably electrocute myself and set both our vehicles on fire.''

"No problem. I appreciate the help. Are you sure I can't repay you by looking at the washer?"

"Thanks, but no. Think of this as part of our service here at Serenity House."

Nash studied her for a few seconds before turning and walking toward the parked cars. Stephanie sighed in relief. While the offer to pay her back was really nice, she had less than no interest in an amateur messing around with her washing machine. Whenever Marty had decided to "help," he ended up completely breaking whatever had only been partially broken before. Now she hired experts at the first sign of trouble. Easier and certainly cheaper in the long run.

She followed Nash to the curb and watched as he popped the hoods on both vehicles. He stretched out the cables and clamped one end to her battery.

"What brings you to Glenwood?" she asked as he walked to his car and she did the same.

"I'm visiting family."

Huh. She wouldn't have picked him for the small-town type. "I don't know anyone named Harmon in the area."

He opened his car door. "Actually their last name is Haynes."

"The Haynes men?"

He frowned slightly. "You know them?"

"Sure. Travis Haynes is our sheriff. Kyle, his brother, is one of the deputies, as is his sister, Hannah." Stephanie tilted her head. "Let me see. I think Hannah is only a half sister. I never heard the whole story. There are a couple more brothers. One's a firefighter and one lives in Fern Hill.''

''You know a lot.''

''Glenwood isn't the big city. It's the sort of place where we all keep track of each other.''

Which was one of the things she liked about the area. While owning a bed and breakfast had never been one of her dreams, if she had to run that kind of business, far better here than somewhere cold and impersonal.

Nash moved into his car and turned the key. The engine caught.

When he stepped back out, Stephanie studied his dark hair and strong jaw. ''I can see the family resemblance,'' she said. ''Are you a cousin?''

''Not exactly.'' He released the jumper-cable connection. ''I don't know much about them. Maybe you could fill me in later.''

A shiver shimmied through her. Anticipation, she realized. Great. In the time it took to serve breakfast and dig out jumper cables, she'd developed a crush. She was thirty-three. Shouldn't she be immune to that kind of foolishness?

He coiled the cables, then handed them to her. ''If it's not too much trouble.''

''Not one bit. Hunt me down when you're ready. I'm usually in the kitchen after the boys get home from school.''

''Thanks.''

He smiled. Unlike last night's, this one reached his eyes. They brightened for a moment, which made the cold foggy morning suddenly less dreary.

Oh, she had it bad. And as soon as her long-legged, hunky guest drove off in his rental car, she was going to give herself a stern talking-to. Falling for one pretty face once had turned her life into a disaster. Did she really want to risk that a second time?

She was a sensible woman with children and bills. The odds of her finding love with a decent responsible guy had to be substantially less than one in a million. She would do well to remember that.

## Chapter Two

Nash circled around Glenwood and started out on the interstate. He checked his watch and when he'd traveled twenty minutes, he drove off at the next exit, turned around and headed back to town.

With his car battery charged, he meandered through the picturesque residential neighborhoods. Ancient trees lined many blocks, the heavy branches touching over the streets and providing tunnels of shade. Big lawns stretched out in front of well-kept houses. Bikes and sports equipment littered the edges of driveways while bright blooming flowers provided color.

The quiet small-town neighborhood wasn't anything like the lakefront in Chicago where he currently lived. No big city lurked in the background. Despite the geographical differences, he was reminded of life back where he'd grown up. Possum

Landing, Texas, might not have been as upscale as Glenwood, but it had the same friendly feel.

He made a couple of turns without any thought of direction. He just wanted to keep moving. Eventually he would have to get in touch with his brother and deal with the pending family reunion, but not just yet.

After his next right turn, he drove onto a wider street lined with huge Victorian houses. They were similar to Stephanie's. All restored, all elegant and framed by massive trees. A discreet sign in front of one indicated it was also a bed and breakfast, with a restaurant. He briefly wondered why Stephanie hadn't opened her business here rather than on the other side of town before dismissing the query and returning his attention to getting lost.

He continued to drive through the neighborhood, turning left, then right. After ten minutes he found himself facing a large shopping mall, which he had driven past the previous evening on his way in from the airport. He was about to turn around when his cell phone rang.

Nash checked the caller ID, then pulled over and hit the Talk button.

"What's up?" he asked, even though he had a good idea of the answer.

"I'm checking on you," Kevin, his twin brother said. "Did you flake out on me at the last minute or are you really here?"

"I'm in town."

"You're kidding."

Kevin sounded surprised. Nash shared the feeling. The last place he'd expected to be was here. Given the choice he would be at work—getting lost in an assignment, or training or even paperwork.

"What changed your mind?" his brother asked.

"I wasn't given a choice. You told me to get my butt here or you'd drag me yourself."

"Right. Like me telling you what to do has made you do anything." Kevin laughed. "I'm glad you made it, though. I've met with a couple of the guys. Travis and Kyle Haynes."

Their half brothers. Family they'd never known about. Nash still couldn't get his mind around the concept. "And?"

"It went great. There's a physical resemblance I didn't expect. Our mutual father has some pretty powerful genes. We're about the same height and build. Dark hair, dark eyes."

Someone said something in the background Nash didn't catch.

Kevin chuckled. "Haley says to tell you they're all good-looking. I wouldn't know about that. It's a chick thing."

Haley? Before Nash could ask, Kevin continued.

"We've set up a dinner for tomorrow night. All the brothers will be there along with their wives and kids. Gage is here."

Gage and Quinn Reynolds had been Nash and Kevin's best friends for as long as they could remember. They'd grown up together. Three weeks ago Nash had found out Gage and Quinn shared their biological father with Nash and Kevin.

"I haven't seen Gage in a couple of years," Nash said. "How's he doing?"

"He's engaged."

"No way."

"Remember Kari Asbury?"

Nash frowned. "The name's familiar."

"He dated her when he left the service and came back to Possum Landing. She took off to New York to be a model or something."

"Oh, yeah. Tall. Pretty. They're getting married?" It had to have been years since they'd seen each other.

"Yup. She moved back and the rest is history. Apparently it all happened pretty fast."

"Even though Gage kept saying he wanted a family, I figured he was going to stay single forever. I hope it works out."

Nash meant it. He wanted his friend to have a happy marriage. To be sure about the woman he married. Not to always wonder what wasn't exactly right between them.

"Gage will be at the dinner tomorrow night," Kevin said. "You're coming, too, right?"

"That's why I'm here." To meet his new family. To try to get involved in something other than work. Maybe to find a way to feel something again.

Was that possible or was he like a kid wishing for the moon?

He didn't want to think about it so he changed the subject. "How's the leg?"

"Good. Healing."

His brother had been shot in the line of duty. Kevin was a U.S. Marshal who had been in the wrong place at the wrong time during a prison riot.

"Do you have a limp?" Nash asked.

"Some, but it's supposed to go away."

"You'll have the scar. Women love scars from

bullet wounds. Knowing you, you'll use it to your advantage.''

"Funny you should say that." Kevin cleared his throat. "I would have told you before, but you were away on assignment. The thing is, I've met somebody.''

Nash thought of the woman's voice he'd heard earlier. "Haley?"

"Yeah. She's…amazing. We're getting married.''

Gage's engagement had been a surprise. Kevin's left Nash speechless. He stared out at the tree-lined streets and couldn't think of a single thing to say.

"You want to meet her?" Kevin asked.

"Sure.''

Why not? His brother had been born wild. Nash figured any woman strong enough to tie Kevin down had to be an amazing combination of sin and steel.

"We're staying at a bed and breakfast in town.''

Kevin named the street and Nash realized it was the one he'd been on a few minutes ago.

"I'm about two miles away," he said. "I'll be right over.''

"A minister's daughter?" Nash said as he stared at Kevin.

His fraternal twin grinned. "Not what you expected?''

"Not even close. What happened to all bad girls all the time?''

His brother shrugged. "I met Haley.''

"That had to have been some meeting.''

Kevin grinned. "It was.''

He motioned to the parlor just to the left of the foyer, then led the way into the formally furnished room. Nash glanced around, noting that this B&B seemed larger and more elegant than Stephanie's. There were crystal chandeliers and some kind of tapestries on the wall. Her place was more homey.

Kevin limped to a long, high-backed sofa in a rich floral print. As he settled onto the cushions, he rubbed his thigh.

Nash took a chair on the opposite side of the coffee table. "You've seen a doctor for that, right?"

"When it happened and again back home. I'm healing. In another few weeks I'll be back to normal, but until then it aches from time to time. I know I'm lucky. The bullet missed the bone."

What he didn't say was if it had hit eighteen inches higher and a little to the left, he wouldn't have made it at all. Nash didn't like to think of anything bad happening to his brother.

"I thought you promised we weren't going to have to worry about you anymore," he said.

Kevin shrugged. "If I hadn't drawn the short straw, I would have been in Florida on a drug bust instead of delivering a prisoner. It wasn't my fault." He grinned. "Not that I'm complaining. If I hadn't been in Kansas, I wouldn't have met Haley."

"A minister's daughter," Nash repeated. "I still can't believe it. So where did you two hook up? Church?"

"A bar."

The answer came from the doorway. Nash turned and saw a young woman walking into the parlor. As he stood he saw she was of medium height, with short fluffy blond hair and hazel eyes. She was pretty enough, curvy, dressed in a snug T-shirt and shorts. His gaze automatically went to her bare legs and he waited for the kind of reaction he'd experienced when he'd seen that sliver of Stephanie's stomach that morning.

Nothing.

Which didn't make sense. If he hadn't had sex in forever and he was finally starting to feel something, why didn't Haley ring any bells?

"You must be Nash," Haley said as she approached. She tilted her head. "Wow—you're tall, like Kevin, and really nice-looking. The same dark hair and dark eyes, but you don't look very much alike." She wrinkled her nose. "What is it with this gene pool? Aren't any of you going to be fat or balding or at least kind of unattractive?"

Kevin beamed at his fiancée. He wrapped an arm around her and brushed a kiss against her temple. "Haley speaks her mind. You'll get used to it."

"If not, I'm sure you're polite enough not to say anything to my face," Haley said cheerfully.

She sank onto the sofa, pulling Kevin next to her. Nash sat down, as well. After linking hands with Kevin, Haley leaned forward and studied Nash.

"I'm really excited about the whole brother-in-law thing," she told him. "I'm an only child. I had way too many mothers, but no siblings. I always wanted other kids around. Some of it was to take the heat off me. I mean I couldn't even think bad thoughts. It's like everyone could read my mind. How awful is that? Okay, sometimes it was really great to have so many people worrying about me, but it could be stifling, too."

Kevin bumped her shoulder with his. "Slow down. You're going to scare Nash off. He's not the sociable twin."

Her gaze became as penetrating as a laser. "Really."

Nash shifted uncomfortably. "Congratulations on your engagement," he said in an effort to distract her. "If Kevin wasn't completely honest about his past, I'd be happy to fill in the details."

Haley giggled with delight. "Ooh, stories about when Kevin was bad. He's told me a few things, but not about the women. There had to be dozens, right? Hundreds, even?"

Now Kevin was the one squirming in his seat. "Haley, you know everything important. I love you. I want to spend the rest of my life with you."

She sighed and rested her head on his shoulder. "Isn't he the best? I can't wait to get married. Speaking of which, are you dating, Nash?"

Kevin stood and pulled Haley to her feet. "I think you've terrorized my brother long enough."

"What?" she asked as she put her hands on her hips. "What did I say?"

He gave her a little push. "I won't be long."

"Did I upset you?" she asked Nash.

He stood. "Not at all. From what I can tell, you're exactly what my brother needs in his life."

"Ha." She tossed her head and walked out of the room. "I'll be upstairs," she called back. "Planning the wedding. A really big wedding."

"Have fun," Kevin said, then flopped back on the sofa. "She's a handful."

Nash sat down. "Interesting young woman."

"I think so. She's smart, funny, fearless. She gives with her whole heart. I'm still learning how to do that, but she makes it so damn easy to love her."

Had that been the problem? Nash wondered. Had

Tina not been easy to love? Had the work got in the way?

"Enough about me," his brother said. "How are you doing?"

"Fine," Nash said. "Great."

Kevin didn't look convinced. "I didn't think it was possible to pry you away from work."

Nash shrugged, rather than admit the vacation hadn't been his idea. "I'm here, ready to meet the family."

"Yeah, right." Kevin's expression turned serious. "You've always been quiet, but since Tina died, it's been worse than usual. Are you coming out of that?"

As Nash had never been willing to acknowledge what he felt about his wife's death, he didn't know if he'd recovered or not. Still it was easier to say, "Sure. I'm doing great."

His brother shook his head. "You still blame yourself. It was never your fault."

"Whose fault was it?"

"Maybe no one's. Maybe it just happened."

"Not on my watch."

"You can't control everything."

Nash knew. The realization was one of the reasons he'd stopped sleeping, stopped eating, stopped living. But knowing that didn't seem to change anything.

"Tell me about the Haynes family," he said to change the subject.

Kevin continued to watch him for a couple of seconds, then nodded, as if agreeing to the tactic. "The couple I've met have been good men. They're as surprised by all this as we are, but friendly enough.'' He smiled. ''They're all cops.''

Nash knew there were four brothers and a sister. ''You're kidding.''

''No. They're all—'' He broke off and laughed. ''Wait. I forgot. One of them is a rebel. He's a firefighter.''

Which wasn't the same as being a cop, but it was close. Kevin was a U.S. Marshal, Gage a sheriff. Nash worked for the FBI and Quinn, well, Quinn walked his own road.

''It's in the blood,'' he said.

Kevin nodded. ''That's what they're telling me. Earl Haynes was sheriff of this town for years. He has a bunch of brothers and they're all in law enforcement. Maybe we're following our destiny.''

Destiny? Nash didn't believe in that kind of crap. He'd gone to work for the FBI because he'd been recruited out of college. Of all the offers he'd received, it was the one that had appealed the most.

''I've seen Gage,'' Kevin said. ''We've known him and Quinn all our lives, played together, fought, made up. I'm having trouble getting that we were always brothers.''

''We acted like brothers,'' Nash said. ''Still, I'm with you. I figured we were good friends, nothing more.''

Did the new knowledge change anything? He wasn't sure.

''The dinner tomorrow night is going to be a zoo,'' Kevin said. ''The guys, their wives and kids. If I can pull together lunch with just a few of the brothers are you interested?''

''Sure.'' Nash didn't like crowds.

Kevin jerked his head toward the ceiling. "There are a few empty rooms. Want to come stay here?"

"I'm okay where I am."

"You sure?"

He knew Kevin thought he was avoiding contact with the world, but that wasn't it at all. If his brother pressed him he would say that packing and unpacking was a pain, which was a lie, but would get him off the hook. The truth was something else. For the first time in two years, he'd actually felt a glimmer of interest in something other than work. He knew his sexual stirrings and physical hunger didn't mean anything, but he was intrigued enough to want to stick around and see what happened next.

Nash hung out with Kevin and Haley until early afternoon, then headed back to Serenity House. When he entered the high-ceilinged foyer, he hesitated, not sure what to do with the rest of his day. As much as he wanted to check in with the office, he knew it was too soon. Calling now would simply prove his boss's point.

He walked through the dining room and into the kitchen. The tidy room was empty. He strolled into the hallway and listened. There was only silence. A quick check of the garage told him what he'd suspected. He was alone.

The knowledge should have relieved him. He didn't like a lot of company, preferring solitude to vapid chatter. He liked the quiet. Only not today. Right now he felt restless and out of place. It was as if his skin had suddenly gotten too small.

He turned toward the stairs and took three steps, then stopped. He didn't want to read or watch TV.

He considered another long drive, but that didn't appeal to him. Finally, in desperation for a distraction, he moved into the back of the house.

In the utility room he found the washer still in pieces. He opened the lid and stared at the tub full of clothes and water, then studied the dial. After skimming the manual, he figured out the washer had stopped right before the spin cycle. He pushed aside the parts and tools, then settled on the floor. There was a schematic of the interior of the machine, along with a parts list. Nash laid the diagram flat on the floor and began sorting through tools and parts.

Over an hour later, Nash had found the problem and, he hoped, fixed it. He'd just started on reassembling the machine when he heard a door slam in the house. The wrench he'd been holding dropped to the floor.

He swore good-naturedly as he picked it up. If he was dropping tools in anticipation of seeing Stephanie, he was in even more trouble than he'd first thought. Finding her sexy was one thing, but actual nerves weren't allowed.

He turned as the footsteps approached, but instead of the petite blonde he'd been expecting, a boy stepped into the room.

Nash remembered the other two kids had been younger and identical twins. So this one would be Stephanie's oldest. He offered a smile.

"Hi, there."

The boy didn't smile back. He folded his arms over his chest and narrowed his eyes as he studied Nash. "You're not the repair guy."

"You're right. I'm Nash Harmon. I'm a guest here."

Nash wiped his hand on a paper towel and held it out. The boy hesitated, then slowly offered his own hand.

"Brett Wynne."

They shook slowly. Nash had the feeling he was being given the once-over and judging from Brett's expression, he wasn't measuring up.

"Why are you messing with our washer?" Brett asked. "Guests aren't supposed to do that sort of thing. If you break it worse, Mom's gonna be real mad. Plus it'll cost more to fix."

The boy looked to be about eleven or twelve. Tall and skinny, with light blond hair and blue eyes like his mother. Of course his father could have had blue eyes, too.

He looked hostile, protective and painfully young. No kid that age should have to feel as if he was all that stood between his family and a hostile world.

Nash carefully set the wrench on the ground. Brett's fierce scowl and hostile words brought back memories from a long time ago. Back when Nash had felt *he* was the one responsible for making sure his mom and brother were safe. The accompanying feelings weren't comfortable.

"You have a point," he said quietly. "I *am* a guest here. The thing is, this morning the battery was dead on my rental car, so your mom gave me a jump. I wanted to pay her back for that. She'd been working on the washer when I found her and asked her to help me. She's a real classy lady, so I knew she wouldn't let me pay her. That's when I thought of the washer."

Brett's expression softened a little, but he didn't

look a whole lot more welcoming. "What if you break it worse?"

"Then I'll pay for the repairs. The point of doing someone a favor is to make her life easier, not more difficult." He casually cleared some space on the vinyl floor covering. "I'm pretty sure I figured out what was wrong with the machine."

"Yeah?" Brett sounded skeptical. "Show me."

Nash scooted back to give the kid a clear view of the machine. "That part back there came loose, which meant this section moved forward. These two pieces got in the way, and this one ended up a little bent."

Brett crouched down and stared as Nash pointed to the problem areas. He explained what he'd done so far and how he was now putting the machine back together.

"I'll stop if you want," he said.

Brett sank onto the floor. His blue eyes widened in surprise. "You mean if I say not to do any more you won't?"

"That's right."

Brett glanced from the washer to Nash and back. "I guess it would be okay for you to finish up. Maybe you haven't made it worse."

High praise, Nash thought, holding in a grin. "Want to help me?"

"Yeah." Brett sounded eager. Then he gave a shrug. "I mean I'm not doing anything else right now."

Nash handed him the wrench and showed him where to tighten the edge of the casing. "Turn that there."

Fifteen minutes later, the washer was nearly back

in one piece. Brett had given up being distant and sullen and now bombarded Nash with questions.

"How'd you figure out what had happened? You ever take a washer apart before?"

"When I was a teenager," Nash told him. "With computer chips and electronics a lot of home appliances are getting pretty complicated, but this washer's older. That made it easier to see what was wrong. Your mom had already taken it apart. I just poked around."

He didn't mention that Stephanie had been trying a combination of guilt and physical abuse on the old machine. Thinking about how she's stopped to kick it as she'd walked out of the room that morning made him smile.

"My bike chain came off once," Brett said. "I got it back on and tightened up some stuff, but I guess that's not the same."

"You're pretty mechanical," Nash told the kid. "You handle these tools well."

Brett pretended nonchalance. "I know."

Just then someone cleared her throat. Nash glanced over his shoulder and saw Stephanie standing in the doorway to the utility room. The twins were right behind her, peering at him from either side of her hips. She didn't look happy.

"I know you're trying to help, Mr. Harmon, but this isn't your responsibility."

Before Nash could speak, Brett scrambled to his feet.

"It's okay, Mom. I think Nash really fixed it. He knows about machines and stuff. We're just putting it back together. Let's test it."

Stephanie's doubt was as clear as her frown. "Brett, the washer isn't a toy."

"Good thing," Nash said as he stood and looked down at her. "Because I wasn't playing."

## Chapter Three

Had she already mentioned that the man was tall? Stephanie had to tilt her head back to meet Nash's dark gaze. Once her eyes locked onto his, she didn't think an earthquake would be enough to break the connection between them.

What exactly was the appeal? His chiseled good looks? The hint of sadness even when he smiled? A body big enough and muscled enough to make him the most popular guy in a "drawing the human form" class? Her sex-free existence? That voice?

*I wasn't playing.*

She knew what he'd meant when he spoke the words. He wasn't playing at being Mr. Repair. He was just trying to help. But she wanted him to mean something else. She wanted him to mean that he thought she was sexy, mysterious and, seeing as this was her personal fantasy, irresistible. She wanted him to mean he wasn't playing with her. He wanted it to be real, too.

Yeah, that and a nod from a genie would miraculously get the piles of laundry clean, too.

"Stephanie? Are you all right?"

Good question.

"Fine."

She forced herself to look away from his face and focus her attention on the nearly assembled washer. The scattered tools on the floor were enough to remind her of Marty, who had loved to play at fixing things. He knew just enough to be dangerous to both himself and her monthly budget. Like she needed that kind of trouble again.

"Tell me exactly what you did," she said. She would need the information to tell the repair guy.

Before Nash could speak, Brett launched into an explanation that involved calling tools by their actual names and pointing out various washer parts on a diagram so detailed, she got vertigo just looking at it. She did her best to pay attention. Really. It was just that the utility room was sort of on the small side and Nash was standing close enough for her to inhale the scent of his shampoo and the faint hint of male sweat. It had been a really long time since she'd seen a man perspire.

And it wasn't going to happen again anytime soon, she told herself firmly. Men, good-looking or not, weren't a part of her to-do list. She was going to put any illicit or illegal thoughts of Nash Harmon right out of her mind.

The bad news was she'd assumed that her reaction to him that morning had come from a lack of caffeine and low blood sugar. As she'd had enough coffee to float a good-size boat and she was still full from lunch, she couldn't blame her current attraction on either of those states. There had to be another explanation.

"Mom, you're not listening," Brett complained.

"I am. You got a little technical on me. I guess it's a guy thing."

She watched as her son tried to decide between being huffy at her inattention and pleasure at her calling him a guy.

"There's a simple way to ease your mind," Nash said.

Reluctantly she looked in his direction, careful not to get caught up in his lethal gaze.

"Let me guess," she said. "You're going to turn it on and prove to me that it works."

"Exactly."

He smiled and staring at that was nearly as dangerous. When his mouth curved, her stomach swooned. The sensation was more than a little disconcerting.

"Okay, let her rip." She bent down to the twins and rested her hands on their shoulders. "You two brace yourselves. If the washer starts to hiss and shake I want you to run for cover. Okay?"

They nodded solemnly.

The three of them watched as Nash closed the lid, then pushed in the dial. There was a second of silence followed by a click. Then, amazingly, the old washer chugged to life. She heard the sound of the tub turning, followed by water gurgling down the drain.

"I don't believe it," she said. "It might actually be working."

Brett grinned. "Mo-om. It *is* working. Nash and I fixed it."

"Wow!" She brushed his cheek with her fingers. "I'm impressed."

Adam tugged on her shirt. "I'm hungry, Mom. I want my afternoon snack."

"Me, too," Jason said.

"Meet me in the kitchen." She turned her attention back to Nash. "I don't know how to thank you. Of course I'll discount your room for the work. The last time the repairman was here, he charged me a hundred dollars."

"Forget it," he said as he crouched down and began collecting tools. "You helped me out this morning. I'm returning the favor."

"Jump-starting your car hardly compares with fixing my washer. I have to pay you something."

He glanced up. "Then I'll take an afternoon snack, too."

That wasn't enough, but it would have to do for now. Brett planted his hands on his hips.

"What do I get?"

"My undying gratitude."

"How about a new skateboard?"

She winced. The one he wanted had special wheels or a secret finish or something that cranked up the price tag to the stratosphere.

"We'll talk," she told her oldest.

"You always say that, but we never have the conversation," he complained as he stalked out of the room.

She watched him go and was pleased when he turned into the kitchen rather than heading toward the stairs and up to his room. Brett was twelve—

nearly a teenager. She didn't want to think about handling a teenage boy all on her own. She didn't like to think about dealing with any of it all on her own. Unfortunately, she didn't have a choice. The past few years had taught her that alone was a whole lot better than marriage to the wrong guy.

She turned back to Nash. "How about coffee and shortbread cookies?"

He finished putting the tools in the box and stood. "Sounds terrific."

"I'll bring them into the dining room in about five minutes."

She started to leave, then stopped. The washer clicked over from spin to rinse. "I still can't believe you fixed that. I have laundry piled up to the ceiling. We've been running out of clothes. I really do appreciate your help."

"I was glad to do it." He leaned against the washer. "My work keeps me pretty busy. I'm not used to having a lot of free time and this gave me something to do."

She laughed. "Uh-huh. Next you'll be telling me I was doing *you* the favor by letting you work on the washer."

"Exactly."

"Nice try, Nash, but I don't buy it."

She headed for the kitchen. Every single cell in her body tingled from their close encounter. Did sexual attraction burn calories? Wouldn't it be nice if it did?

She started a fresh pot of coffee, then got out glasses for the boys. Brett poured the milk while she set out grapes, string cheese and a plate of cookies. By the time that was done, the coffee had finished.

She poured it into a carafe, then set it on the tray, along with shortbread cookies, grapes and some crab puffs she'd been defrosting.

"Be right back," she told her children as she picked up the tray and walked toward the dining room.

Nash stood by the front window, staring out onto the street. When she entered, he turned and smiled. "Thanks."

"You're welcome." She put down the tray. "Let me know if you need anything else."

"I will."

She would like to tell herself that he was talking about more than just the food. While she was busy imagining that, she could pretend that his gaze lingered on her face and that his relaxed stance belied pulsing erotic tension building just below the surface of his calm facade. Or she could be realistic and get her fanny back to the kitchen.

Being reasonably intelligent, she chose the latter and left Nash in peace. The poor man hadn't asked for her sudden rush of hormones. If she didn't want to embarrass them both, she was going to have to find a way to get her wayward imagination under control. If logic wasn't going to work, she was going to have to think of more drastic measures.

"Tell me about school," she said as she slid onto the chair between Adam and Jason.

Her twins were in third grade, while Brett had just finished his first year in middle school.

"Mrs. Roscoe said we're her best class ever," Adam told her. "We beat all the other classes." He gave his twin a triumphant grin.

Jason ignored him. "We got our summer reading

lists today, Mom,'' he said. ''I've picked out five books already. Can we go to the library this week?''

''Sure. You'll all want to think about summer reading. We're going to have to talk about how many books you'll be getting through. Are there book reports?''

Adam reached for the backpack he'd left on the floor and pulled out a folder. He passed a single sheet of paper to her.

Stephanie scanned the directions, then glanced at Brett. ''What about you?''

He rolled his eyes. ''It's up in my room. We have to do about two pages. I want to do mine on the computer. Are we getting a new one? You said we'd talk about it when school was out.''

''You're right. And unless I'm reading the calendar wrong, school isn't out yet.''

''We've got four days left.''

''Which gives me ninety-six hours until you can start bugging me.''

Brett tried to hide his smile, but she saw it. He'd been after her for a new computer for the better part of a year. While there was nothing wrong with the one they had, it didn't play the really cool games. She figured she could probably put him off until Christmas when her ''twenty dollars a week'' fund would have reached computer size. Then the new computer would be a family gift.

Adam bounced in his chair. ''I have a new joke,'' he announced. ''Knock knock.''

''Those are baby jokes,'' Brett said as he took a cookie.

''They are age-appropriate,'' Stephanie told him. ''I listened to yours when you were his age.''

Brett sighed, then dutifully went through the joke with his brother who squealed with delight when he repeated the word *who* enough for Adam to ask him why he was being an owl. Jason giggled at his older brother.

As the three of them took turns talking about their day, Stephanie found her attention sliding to the man in the next room. He was sitting out there alone while she was in here with her family. She kept having to fight the impulse to invite him to join them. Which was crazy. She'd never once encouraged guests to befriend her children. Besides, if Nash was alone, it was by choice.

He was probably married, she told herself. Or he had a serious girlfriend back in Chicago. She knew he had family here—he'd mentioned the Hayneses, although not how he was related to them.

Indecision made her fidget in her seat until she couldn't stand it anymore.

''I'll be right back,'' she told the boys and stalked out of the room.

This was insane, she told herself. She was asking for trouble. Worse, she was asking for humiliation. She needed therapy.

As there was no psychologist standing by to offer advice, she walked into the dining room only to find Nash where she'd last seen him. Standing in front of the window looking out onto the street.

A quick glance at the tray told her he hadn't touched the food she'd brought him. He hadn't even poured any coffee.

He turned around and raised his eyebrows in silent query.

After clearing her throat, she tried to figure out

what to say. Nothing brilliant occurred to her so she was left with slightly awkward.

"You must miss your family," she said.

His eyebrows lowered and drew together. "I haven't met them yet."

What? Oh. "I meant your family in Chicago."

"I don't have any there. I'm not married."

Score one for the hormones, she thought, trying not to feel or look relieved. The good news was that when Nash left, she would have a great time remembering all the surging feelings she'd experienced while he was here. It would be a lot more interesting than sorting coupons or ironing.

"Okay." She sucked in a breath. "You can tell me no. It's completely crazy and not even why you're here. I don't usually even ask. Why would you want to?" She shook her head. "Forget it."

She took a step back.

He blinked at her. "Was there a question in there for me?"

"I don't think so." She waved toward the kitchen. "We're just hanging out in there. The boys tell me about their day at school and they have a snack. You seemed…" She tried a different line of thought. "You're welcome to join us if you'd like. Or you can simply run screaming from the room and I'll get the message."

He looked surprised, and not exactly comfortable with the idea. Of course. He was a sexy, successful, single guy. Men like that didn't hang out with three kids and a single mom.

Heat crawled up her cheeks and she had a bad feeling there was a blush to match. "Never mind," she said brightly. "It was a silly suggestion."

She started toward the closed door that led to the kitchen, but before she'd gone more than two steps, he called her back.

"I would like to join you," he said.

She eyed him. "Why?"

He smiled and her internal organs did a couple of synchronized swimming moves.

"Because you asked and it sounds like fun."

"I'm not sure about fun, but I can promise loud."

"Close enough."

Now that he'd accepted, she felt foolish about her invitation, but it was too late to retract it. She moved to the table and collected the tray, then tilted her head in the direction of the kitchen.

"Brace yourself," she said and pushed open the door with her shoulder.

All three of her boys were talking at once. They barely noticed her, but the second Nash walked in behind her three pairs of blue eyes widened and three mouths snapped closed.

"This is Mr. Harmon," she said as she put the tray on the counter.

"Nash," he said easily.

"Okay. Nash. These are my boys. You've already met Brett, who is rapidly becoming a macho tool guy. And these two—" She walked to the table and put her hands on their shoulders. "—are my twins. Jason and Adam. Say hi to Nash."

The twins offered an enthusiastic greeting, but Brett didn't say much. His expression turned wary and Stephanie wondered if he was about to say something that would make her cringe.

"We're having chocolate chip cookies, grapes and string cheese," she said quickly in an effort to forestall Brett. "You're welcome to that or the shortbread."

"How about shortbread and grapes," he said.

"No problem."

As she bustled around the kitchen, he pulled out one of the two empty chairs. Brett sat across from the twins, which meant Nash would be across from her. It was only a snack, she told herself. She could handle it. At least she hoped she could.

As she worked, she tried not to notice the silence. Her normally ten-thousand-words-a-minute kids were all staring at Nash. But before she could think of something to ease the escalating tension, Nash broke the ice himself.

He leaned toward Jason and Adam. "I'm a twin," he said.

The boys grinned. "No way," Jason said.

"Not identical, like you two. Kevin and I don't look very much alike. But we're still twins."

"Cool." Adam offered a shy smile.

Nash turned to Brett. "I heard school is out this week. Are you excited about summer?"

Stephanie saw her oldest wrestle with his innate excitement and his need to be standoffish.

"Summer's good," Brett said at last.

"There's a community pool," Jason said. "We go swimming every week. And there's sleepover camp at the end of summer. And Adam and me are gonna play volleyball at the park."

"Sounds like fun," Nash said.

"Brett's seriously into baseball," Stephanie volunteered as she carried a plate to the table, then returned to collect the coffee. "His team made the city finals."

"What position do you play?" Nash asked.

"First base."

She could see he was itching to say more, but for some reason didn't want to. As if wanting to talk to Nash was a bad thing.

Stephanie sighed. Brett considered himself the "man of the family." He took his responsibilities seriously. While she appreciated the effort, sometimes she wished she could convince him that it was far more important to her for him just to be a kid.

Conversation flowed for about twenty minutes until she glanced at the empty plates in front of her three. "Looks like you're done eating to me. Guess what comes next?"

Adam smiled shyly at Nash. "We do our homework now."

"It's when I used to do it, too," he admitted. "I liked every subject but English. What about you?"

"I like 'em all," Jason announced and pushed back his chair.

He carried his plate to the counter by the sink, then gave Stephanie a hug. She hugged him back. As she felt his small back and warm, tugging hands, she reminded herself that jerk or not, Marty had done one thing right. He'd given her these boys. They were worth all the heartache and suffering she'd endured along the way.

When all three of them had trooped out of the kitchen, she turned to the table. Nash would go now, she thought. Which was fine. She'd tortured him with her family long enough. Whatever feelings of loneliness he might have had would have been erased. No doubt he would be grateful for some solitude.

"Good cookies," he said as he rose.

"Thanks. I won't tell you how much butter is in each batch."

"I appreciate that."

He carried his plate and mug over to the sink, which was a bit of a surprise. Then, before she could say anything, he turned on the water and began to rinse them off.

Stephanie thought about rubbing her eyes. She had to be having some kind of hallucination. A man? Doing work? Not in her world.

"You don't have to do that," she said, trying not to sound stunned.

"I don't mind helping."

As he spoke, he collected the boys' plates and rinsed those off, too. Then he opened the dishwasher and actually put the plates inside. She couldn't believe it. She didn't think Marty had ever known where the dishwasher was, let alone what it was for.

When Nash reached for the glasses, she came to her senses.

"Hey, I'm the hired help around here, not you," she said as she stepped in close and took the glass from him.

Their fingers touched. Just for a second, but it was enough. Not only did she hear the faint ringing of bells, she would swear that she saw actual sparks arc between them. Holy wow. Sparks. She didn't think that kind of stuff was possible after age thirty.

Nash looked at her. His dark eyes seemed bright with what she wanted to say was passionate fire, but was probably the light from the overhead fixtures. Awareness rippled through her, sensitizing her skin and making her want to fling herself into his arms for a kiss that went on for at least six hours, following by mindless, intense sex. Right there, in front of the appliances.

She swallowed and took a step back. Something was really wrong with her. Seasonal allergies? Too much television? Not enough? She felt soft and wet and achy inside. She felt unsettled. All of this was so out of the ordinary, so unexpected and so extreme that it would be really hilarious…if it weren't so darned terrifying.

Nash wondered if Stephanie really was issuing an invitation with her parted lips and wide eyes or if that was just wishful thinking on his part. No doubt the latter, he told himself as he heard footsteps on the stairs.

The boys walked into the kitchen. Adam and Jason each had a backpack with them while Brett carried a math book and several sheets of paper.

Nash figured it was time for him to excuse himself. Homework seemed like family time. But before he could say anything, Jason patted the chair next to him and offered a winning smile.

"I have to finish my calendar for summer. I wrote something about each of the months. Wanna hear?"

Nash glanced from the boy to Stephanie who gave him a shrug, as if to say it was his call. When he looked back at Jason, the boy pulled the chair out a little.

What the hell, Nash thought. He crossed to the table and took the seat.

"So your calendar is only three months long," he said.

"Uh-huh. We did pictures. See—I colored

fireworks in the sky for July, coz that's when it's the fourth and we always go to the park for fireworks.''

Jason opened a large folder and withdrew a folded sheet of construction paper as he spoke. Nash admired the crayon depiction of fireworks, then bent close to see what Jason had written underneath.

''It's a poem,'' the boy said proudly. ''The teacher said we could copy it from the board if we wanted. I can read it to you.''

The last sentence sounded more like a question than a statement. Nash nodded. ''Sure. Go ahead.''

Jason cleared his throat, then read the poem. When he was finished Adam quietly pushed a spelling list toward him.

''I got 'em all right,'' he said in a low voice.

Nash studied the word list, and the big *A* at the top of the paper.

''You did great. There are some big words here.''

Adam beamed.

The twins pulled out more papers and talked about their homework. When they'd explained everything they had to do, they started the work. But it wasn't a silent process. They asked questions, shared each step, bickered over the pencil sharpener and asked for more snacks, another glass of milk or even water. Stephanie kept gently steering them back to their assignments.

''They're usually more focused than this,'' she said as she pulled food out of the refrigerator. ''The last couple of weeks of school are always crazy.''

Nash remembered what that was like—the unbearable anticipation of an endless summer with no homework. Being here with the boys reminded him of a lot of things. How he and Kevin were supposed to do their homework as soon as they got home, but with their mom out working, there was no one around to make sure it happened. Nash had always done his, but Kevin had usually ducked outside to play. Later, when their mom got home, they fought about it. Nash had retreated to his room to get lost in a book.

As he glanced at the three bent heads, he realized he didn't have any children in his life. No kids of friends, no neighbors with little ones running around. He couldn't remember the last time he'd spent any time with a child. It wasn't that he didn't like them; they simply weren't a part of his world.

Had someone asked him what it would be like to spend an hour or so with three boys, he would have assumed time would go by slowly, that he would feel awkward and restless. But his usual underlying sense that something was wrong seemed to have faded. The twins were friendly enough and while Brett obviously didn't want him around, Nash understood enough of what he was feeling not to mind. When Nash had been his age, he'd done exactly the same thing.

Stephanie came over and put her hand on Brett's shoulder. "How's it going?"

"Fine."

Nash wasn't sure that was true. Brett hadn't written anything on his paper in nearly ten minutes.

Stephanie smiled at Nash. "Brett is in an accelerated math group. He's already starting on algebra, and it's a little tough. Unfortunately I was never a math person. Still, he's way better at it than me."

Brett winced. "Mo-om, I'm doing fine."

"I know, honey. You're doing great."

Nash glanced down at the open book. "I remember algebra," he said.

She drew her eyebrows together. "Let me guess. You *were* a math person."

"Sorry, yeah."

"Figures."

"The thing I always liked about it was the rules. Once you learn them, you keep applying them. Things need to happen in a certain order, otherwise you get the wrong answer."

She shook her head. "That would be me. The queen of the wrong answer. It was all that do-this-first stuff that made me crazy. Why can't you just do an equation from left to right, like reading?"

"You can. Sort of. Like this problem here." He pointed. "You do what's in the parentheses first, then go from left to right."

"Why?"

"Because that's how the steps work. If you're building a model car and you glue down the hood before you put in the engine, it's not going to look right."

She groaned. "Is this where I tell you I can't put a model together, either?"

Brett tapped his pencil on the table. "Can I have my book back, please."

"Sure."

Nash handed it over. At that moment Adam claimed his attention to discuss what color green would do best on his mountains for his report on Wyoming. As Nash checked out the various options, he saw Brett read the first problem again, then start writing on his paper. When he'd finished his calculations, he plugged the answer back into the original equation and quickly solved it. His wide smile told Nash that he'd gotten it right.

Nash handed Adam a colored pencil, then caught Stephanie's eyes. She mouthed ''thank you.'' Apparently she'd picked up his attempt to help Brett without actually helping. Her gaze darkened slightly as several emotions skittered across her face.

He tried to read them, but they came and went in a heartbeat. He was left with a sense of sorrow, as if she had something she regretted.

Of course she did, he told himself. Everyone did. Regrets were a part of life. But for the first time in a long time, he wanted to ask another person what was wrong. He wanted to learn more about her, to understand what she was thinking. He wanted to connect.

His interest was more than sexual and that scared the crap out of him. Feeling—getting involved— would be a disaster.

He told himself to get out of there right now. To leave before he got trapped. Before it was too late. But even knowing it was wrong to stay, he couldn't seem to force himself to stand and walk away.

It was just a couple of hours, he told himself. What could it possibly hurt?

## Chapter Four

Nash stayed through dinner. Stephanie had no idea why, nor could she decide if it was a good thing or a bad thing. The man was nice enough, the twins already adored him even though Brett remained standoffish. She appreciated the opportunity to converse with an adult for a chance. So the situation should have been a big plus.

Except she didn't know what was in it for him. Why would a good-looking, intelligent man want to hang out with her and her kids? She opened the refrigerator and put the milk and butter back in the door, then frowned. That didn't sound exactly right. Nash's appearance and mental state didn't have anything to do with her confusion. Why would *any* man not be running for the hills? Weren't guys supposed to hate other men's children in a relationship? Not that he had any designs on her. Despite the fact that he made her long for satin sheets and champagne, she doubted he saw her as much more than an efficient hostess. After all, her luck just plain wasn't good enough to hope for more.

So why had he stayed? Why hadn't he retreated to the quiet and privacy of his room or gone out somewhere for dinner?

You could ask, a small voice in her head whispered.

Stephanie nearly laughed out loud. Sure she could, but that was so not her style.

"We're done," Brett said.

She turned around and saw that the table was indeed cleared, the dishes scraped and neatly stacked by the sink and the table wiped off.

"Very nice job," she said. "Everyone finished his homework, right?"

Three heads nodded earnestly.

She smiled. "Then I guess this is a TV night."

"All right!"

Brett pumped the air with his fist. The twins tore out of the kitchen. She heard their footsteps on the hardwood floor and was able to guess their destination.

"Stop right there," she yelled after them. "We have a guest. Use the TV upstairs."

"Why?" Nash asked from where he leaned against the counter.

She turned toward him, ignoring the continual sexual impact of his presence. Not only did she not want to make a fool of herself, but there was still a minor in the room. "The downstairs TV is for our guests."

He gave her a slow, sexy smile that could have

melted the polar ice cap. "I'm not much of a TV watcher. It won't bother me if it won't bother you."

Stephanie figured she wasn't going to fight the point. If the man wanted to be generous, her kids would be thrilled. She smiled at Brett. "Looks like this is your lucky day. Go tell your brothers, and keep the volume down."

Brett grinned and raced down the hall. "We can stay down here," he yelled.

"Simple pleasures," she said as she turned toward the sink. "If only life stayed that easy."

"Complicated comes with growing up," Nash said as he also approached the sink. He was closer so he got there first.

As she watched, he turned on the water and began rinsing dishes. Just like that. He even used the sponge to clean off the worst bits.

Stephanie wanted to pinch herself to see if she was dreaming. He was helping again. *Helping.* Without being asked, without complaining. Just doing it.

Some of her confusion must have shown on his face because he looked at her and asked, "What's wrong?"

She wiggled her fingers toward the dishes. "You don't have to do that."

"I don't mind."

He didn't mind. Wow. Every time she had asked Marty to help, he'd howled like a wet cat, then had a list of fifty reasons why he couldn't. However hard she pushed, he pushed back harder. He threatened, cajoled, or had a temper tantrum to rival a three-year-old's. His goal had been to make the experience so miserable that she would stop asking. Eventually it had worked.

"So who trained you?" she asked. "I happen to know that most men aren't born being so handy around the kitchen."

He finished rinsing the dishes, then opened the dishwasher and began placing them inside. "I was married for a while, but most of my 'training' as you call it, came from being raised by a single mom. She worked a lot of hours and came home beat. I pitched in to help."

Wow times two. "You give me hope," she said.

He straightened. "In what way?"

For once her reaction wasn't about sex. "You seem like a great guy. Successful, articulate, not a serial killer—at least not as far as I can tell. You didn't have a father around, either. So maybe my boys will turn out okay, too."

He gave her another slow smile. "They're going to be great. You're doing a terrific job with them."

"I try."

"It shows."

The compliment left her feeling flustered and fluttery. She had to clear her throat before she could speak again. "If you don't mind me asking, what happened in your marriage?"

He put the last three glasses into the dishwasher. "Tina passed away a couple of years ago."

"I'm sorry."

The words were automatic. She figured Nash was in his early thirties, which meant his wife would have been around the same age. What would have taken such a young woman? Cancer? A drunk driver?

"What brought you to Glenwood?" he asked. "Or are you a native?"

The not-so-subtle change in subject ended any thought she had of actually asking her questions.

"Dumb luck," she said.

Nash picked up the dishcloth and rinsed it, then started to wipe off the counters. She was nearly dumbstruck. Rather than stand around with her mouth open, she forced herself to get the detergent out from under the sink and pour some into the dishwasher.

"We always moved around a lot," she said, trying not to stare as he finished up with the counters. "Marty had wonderful ideas of fun places to live and we wanted to experience them all."

Not exactly the whole truth, she thought sadly. This was the made-for-TV version of her marriage. The one she told mostly everyone. Especially her children.

"We spent eight months living in a forest and nearly a year working on a ranch. There was a summer on a fishing boat and a winter in a lighthouse."

Nash leaned against the counter and folded his arms over his chest. "With the kids?"

"It was a great experience for them," she said, trying to sound enthusiastic when all she felt was tired. "They have great memories."

All good ones. She'd done her best to ensure that. Whatever her feelings about her late husband might be, she wanted Brett and the twins to remember their father with a lot of love and laughter.

"I experienced worlds I didn't know existed." And would have happily died in ignorance of, given the choice. She pushed the Delay button on the dishwasher, setting the start time for midnight.

"I'd homeschooled Brett through third grade, which went well. He's very bright. But Marty and I were worried about socialization. We knew it was time to settle down."

It hadn't exactly gone that way, she remembered. Marty had wanted to keep moving, but she'd demanded that they settle. Despite having an eight-year-old and four-year-old twins, she'd flat-out told him she would leave him if necessary. The previous winter Adam had spiked a 105-degree fever while they'd been stuck in the godforsaken lighthouse. With a storm raging around them, there'd been no way to get to the mainland and a doctor. She'd spent thirty-six hours in hell, wondering if her son was going to die. In the dark hours before dawn, right before his fever finally broke, she'd vowed she wasn't going to live like that anymore.

"As luck would have it, the day we arrived in Glenwood we got word of an inheritance. We fell in love with the town right as we found out we had enough money to buy a place and settle down." She offered a practiced smile. "This house was on the market and we couldn't resist. It was the perfect opportunity to have both a home and a growing business."

Nash glanced around at the remodeled kitchen. "You've done a great job."

"Thanks."

What she didn't tell him was that there was a mortgage on the old Victorian house. She also didn't mention the fights she'd had with Marty. There'd been enough money to buy a regular house outright

instead of this place, but that had been too boring
for him. As the inheritance had come from his side
of the family, she hadn't felt she was in a position
to argue too much.

"It was all coming together," she said. "We
closed escrow and started the remodeling. The boys
started school. We were just settling into the community when Marty passed away."

His dark gaze settled on her face. "So it's been
a while."

"About three years. Marty was killed in a car
accident."

"Leaving you with three children. That had to be
tough."

She nodded slowly because agreement was the
expected response. It's not that she'd wished Marty
ill, and she certainly hadn't wanted him dead, yet
by the time he was killed, any love she'd ever felt
had long since died. Only obligation had remained.

"Brett mourned the most of the boys," she said.
"The twins were only five. They have some memories and Brett tells them stories, but it's not very
much. I wish they had more."

She meant that. What did it matter if Marty had
refused to grow up and be responsible? He was still
the boys' father. She wanted them to remember him
as fun and loving. To think the best of him.

"You're doing great," he said. "They're good
kids."

"No potential serial killers?"

"Not a one."

"I hope they're okay. I worry about them growing up without a father. I was an only child, so my
experience with boys was limited to those I knew in

school. I'm trying to encourage the whole 'be ma-cho' thing, while still keeping them on this side of civilized.''

''You mean no spitting indoors?''

She shuddered, then grinned. ''Exactly. No spit-ting, no writing on the walls, no dead animals' skins.''

''Pretty strict rules.'' One corner of his mouth twitched slightly. ''How about a couple of skulls?''

''Animal or human?''

''Does it matter?''

''Of course. Animal is fine, as long as they're small and we bought them from a store. I want clean skulls.''

''Typical girl. Dirt is fun.''

''Easy for you to say. You're not stuck doing the vacuuming.''

Nash dropped his hands to his side and took a step toward her. Just one step, but her breath caught as if she'd just climbed a mountain. He was closer. Much closer. The light mood their conversation had created suddenly thickened. Air refused to flow into her lungs. She felt hot, shivery and more than a little out of control.

When his eyes darkened, she told herself it was a trick of the light, nothing more. It had to be that, because thinking that Nash might also be feeling some flicker of sexual attraction was more than she ever hoped for. It was also outside the realm of pos-sibility.

She wanted to throw herself into his arms and beg him to kiss her. She wanted to rip off her shirt and bra, baring her breasts. Surely that would be enough of a hint. Not that he would be interested in her breasts. She'd had three kids and parts of her were not as perky as they once had been. Miracles could be worked with an underwire bra.

So she could just rip off her shirt and leave the bra on. Still a good hint for him.

Right, she thought with humorous resignation. He would respond by ripping off his shirt, too, right after he wrote her that check for a million dollars.

"I don't want to keep you," she said at last. It was the mature thing to say. The right thing. How disappointing when he nodded.

"I'll see you in the morning."

"I'll be the one baking," she said, keeping her voice light.

He smiled, then walked out of the room. She allowed herself a last look at his rear, then pulled out a kitchen chair and sank onto the seat.

She had to get a grip. Yes, the attraction was nice. The quivery feelings reminded her that she wasn't dead yet. All delightful and completely meaningless messages when compared with the fact that men were nothing but trouble and getting involved with one would make her an idiot times two. Oh sure, she'd heard rumors that there were male members of the species who were actually helpful, responsible and on occasion behaved like partners, but she'd never experienced it firsthand. What were the odds of her encountering one at this point in her life? Even more important, what were the odds of her encountering one in someone who made her hormones belly dance in supplication?

"Is he gone?"

She looked up and saw Brett entering the kitchen. "By 'he' I assume you mean Nash?"

Her twelve-year-old nodded.

"He went up to his room."

Brett pulled out a chair and sat next to her. "Why's this guy hanging around?"

"Maybe he's a film producer doing research on the perfect American family."

Brett rolled his eyes.

Stephanie grinned. "Do you have a better answer?"

"No, but it's totally weird."

"I think it's nice. Don't forget, he fixed our very temperamental washer. The piles of laundry stretching to the ceiling and I are grateful." She touched Brett's shoulder. "You helped him with that. I thought you liked him."

Her son shrugged.

What was going on? Did Brett feel threatened by Nash in some way? Stephanie hadn't dated since Marty's death. Maybe having another guy around made him feel as though his father was being replaced.

"Hey, don't sweat it," she said, leaning close and wrapping her arms around him. "Nash is a guest here. Which means his home is somewhere else and he's going to be leaving us in a couple of weeks. In the meantime, he's nice, he cleans up after himself and I like having another grown-up to talk to. Nothing more. Okay?"

As they were alone, Brett burrowed into her embrace. He'd reached the stage where he didn't allow hugs and kisses in front of other people, but when it was just the two of them, he was still her little boy. Sort of.

He raised his head and looked at her. "Do you still miss Dad?"

She studied his dark blue eyes and the mouth shaped just like Marty's. "Of course I do. I loved him very much."

Brett nodded, as if reassured.

Stephanie told herself that under the circumstances, the lie didn't matter. Her first responsibility was to make her children's world as safe and stable as possible. A dark stain on her conscience was a small price to pay for that.

The teenaged waitress stared at the four men at the table. "I'm new in town," she told them, "but I have to tell you there's something pretty amazing in the water. You're Haynes brothers, aren't you? I recognize you from what I've been told. Every one of you is tall, dark and delicious. You guys all married? Anyone want my number?"

Nash was less surprised by the unsubtle come-on than he would have been before meeting Travis and Kyle Haynes. Kevin had arranged for the four of them to meet up for lunch. Even if he hadn't known about the relationship between them all, he would have guessed something was up the second he saw them.

The four men were nearly identical in height and build. Their dark hair was the same shade and the shapes of their eyes and mouths were similar. Travis and Kyle were a few years older, but still obviously related.

"Thanks, but not today," Kyle said as he took the menus from the young waitress.

"Your loss," she said.

"Probably, darlin', but you should stick to guys your own age."

"What about the stuff they say about older men knowing their way around a woman?"

Kyle grinned. "All lies."

"Why don't I believe you?" She gave a sassy wink, took their drink order and headed off.

Kevin shook his head. "Friendly girl."

Travis Haynes unrolled his paper napkin and set his flatware on the table. "Our family has something of a reputation in this town. Four generations of Haynes men have had their way with a large percentage of the local female population. The four of us have tried to change things, but that sort of legend doesn't die easily."

"Apparently not," Nash said. He looked at his twin. "We don't have a reputation in Possum Landing. We must have been doing something wrong."

"Or right," Kyle said. "Being good with women isn't something to be proud of. Now being a good husband and father—that's a hell of a lot more important."

"Agreed," Travis said. He looked across the table at Nash. "Are you settled in?"

"Yeah. I'm staying at a B&B on the other side of town."

"Stephanie Wynne's place," Kyle said. "Her oldest boy is friends with my oldest son." He smiled. "It's a small town. There aren't many strangers and even fewer secrets."

Travis passed out the menus. "Everything's good here. I'd recommend the burgers, but then I'm a man of simple tastes."

Kevin looked at Nash, then back at Travis. "We're not exactly sushi eaters ourselves."

Kyle leaned forward. He and his brother wore identical khaki uniforms. Travis's name badge proclaimed him sheriff, while Kyle's said he was a deputy.

"Are you two finding this as strange as we are?" Kyle asked.

"Discovering family after all this time?" Nash opened the menu, then closed it. "We had no idea our father had any other children."

"It was one thing to find out that our best friends were actually half brothers," Kevin said. "But when Gage told us about all of you, I was surprised."

The waitress reappeared with their drinks. All the men had ordered iced tea. She took their orders—four burgers, hold the onions, and fries, then disappeared.

"There are five of us," Travis said. His dark brows drew together in a frown. "We have a half sister—Hannah. She works at the sheriff's office, too. She's in communications. Her mother is Louise, who—" He shook his head. "This is going to be confusing as hell."

"Talk slow," Kevin said.

Kyle chuckled. "Travis is good at that—what with being mentally challenged."

Travis turned to his brother. "I can still take you."

"With what army?"

Their playful banter reminded Nash of his relationship with Kevin. Warm, affection and constant.

"There are four Haynes brothers," Travis said.

"Craig's the oldest. He lives in Fern Hill with his wife, Jill, and their five children."

Nash had taken a drink of his iced tea and nearly choked. "Five?"

Travis grinned. "We have a lot of kids. I'm married to Elizabeth. We have four girls. Next is Jordan. He's married to Holly. They have three girls."

"I'm the youngest boy in the family," Kyle said. "I'm married to Sandy. We have five kids, too. Four girls, one boy. Hannah's our half sister, through our father, so she's your half sister, as well. She's married to Nick. They have two girls." He turned to Kevin. "You and Haley are staying at the B&B Nick owns with Louise, Hannah's mother."

Nash set down his glass. "I'm never going to keep this straight."

"It'll get easier with time," Travis said. "There's also Austin Lucas, who isn't officially one of the Haynes men. He's sort of an adopted member of the family. He and his wife, Rebecca, have four kids, three boys and a girl."

"Wait until we start telling you which kids are from a previous marriage," Kyle said.

Kevin held up his hands. "I don't think I want to know."

Nash tried to do the math to figure out how many people could show up at the dinner that night, but lost count somewhere after twenty.

"That's a lot of family members," he said. "Kevin told me your father doesn't live around here." He shook his head. "I guess he's our father, too. I don't think of him that way yet."

Kyle and Travis glanced at each other. "He's in Florida with wife number six or seven," Travis said.

"I've lost count. None of us stay in touch with him."

"Why?" Kevin asked.

"He's..." Travis hesitated. "He wasn't a great father to us."

Nash leaned forward. "Don't worry about offending us with anything you say about him. As far as Kevin and I are concerned, Earl Haynes is just a guy who got a seventeen-year-old virgin pregnant and then walked out on her."

"That was Dad's style," Kyle said quietly. "He was chronically unfaithful. He and his brothers believed that if they slept in their own beds at night, that was about as good as it had to get. They didn't worry about details like being true to one woman or giving a damn about their kids."

"We wanted to be different," Travis told them. "Each of my brothers and I knew how unhappy we'd been and we were determined to keep history from repeating itself. After three generations of bastards, we wanted to make something of our lives, to get involved with our wives and kids. To be good men."

Kyle chuckled. "To have daughters."

"Why would that matter?" Nash asked.

The waitress arrived with their burgers. Once they were served, Kyle reached for the mustard in the center of the table.

"Until Travis and Elizabeth got married," Kyle said, "there hadn't been a girl born to a Haynes man in four generations."

"Not counting Hannah," Travis said. "We didn't know about her." He glanced at Nash.

"Right. Okay, no girls except for Hannah."

"Travis and Elizabeth had a daughter. Then Sandy and me, then Craig and Jill," Kyle said. "Holly and Jordan were next. He's the one who came up with the theory."

"Which is?" Kevin asked.

"Haynes men can only have girls when they're in love with the woman."

"That's crazy," Nash said.

"There's a lot of female Hayneses running around," Travis pointed out. He nodded at Kevin. "Just you wait until you and Haley are having kids."

Kevin grinned. "I look forward to our children, whatever their gender."

"Good," Kyle said, "Because you're probably going to have a lot of them."

## Chapter Five

Nash left the diner after lunch and headed back for the B&B. He'd enjoyed meeting his half brothers, although he found the thought of their large families overwhelming. Five kids. That seemed like a lot.

He'd never much thought about having or not having kids of his own. After marrying Tina, he'd wanted to wait for a while before they started a family. She'd pressured him, but he'd refused to agree. Not until things were more stable between them. He'd assumed there would be children in his future, but when he thought about them they were vague shadows playing on the field at some sporting event. Not real people. Not like Stephanie's kids.

Thinking about Brett, Adam and Jason reminded him of the previous evening. He'd enjoyed helping with homework and staying for dinner. The boys were a lot of fun, each with a distinct personality.

Brett was still waiting to accept him, but Nash respected that. Jason was ready to charm the world while Adam was shyer. As for Stephanie…

Better not to go there, he told himself. As it was, he'd had a restless night filled with erotic dreams of his hostess. He couldn't remember the last time he'd awakened so damn hard. Not since he was a teenager and in the throes of adolescent hormones. Back then he'd had lots of desire but little knowledge about what was supposed to happen between a man and a woman. Now he knew exactly what he wanted to do to and with Stephanie, should he ever get her in his bed.

He grinned as he realized a bed wasn't required. He'd been pretty creative in his dreams. Based on what he remembered, he could happily make love with her just about anywhere. One particularly vivid nocturnal event had been of him holding her up against a wall. She'd wrapped her bare legs around him and he'd—

He groaned as heat and pressure poured into his groin. Determined not to arrive back at the B&B with a hard-on the size of Argentina, he concentrated on the road and forced himself to think about how the houses lining the streets would look if they were all painted green.

The distraction nearly worked. By the time he pulled up in front of the B&B, he was no longer hard, although a dull ache lingered. It throbbed in time with his heartbeat. Experience told him it would go away…eventually.

He climbed out of his rental car and started toward the large house. As he walked along the path, he heard sounds coming from a small gatehouse by the driveway. The front door was open.

Nash changed directions. When he reached the gatehouse, the faint sounds became a song on the radio. He followed the music into an empty living room in the midst of being sanded and patched. Stephanie stood in a doorway about fifteen feet away. She had a piece of sandpaper in each hand.

That morning she'd been dressed in what he thought of as her "public" clothes. Tailored slacks, a dark pink sweater. While he'd been gone, she'd changed into jeans and a T-shirt. A scarf covered her head.

As he watched, she reached up and rubbed at a spot well above her head. Her T-shirt rode up, exposing a bit of stomach. Instantly his groin sprang to life. What was it about this woman and her belly? Shouldn't he be finding her breasts erotic, or even her legs?

"You need a ladder," he said conversationally.

She jumped and squeaked, then glared at him. "I have to go to the grocery store in the next couple of days. I swear I'm going to swing through the pet department and buy you a collar with a bell."

"It's not going to fit."

"I'll put it around your wrist."

"You'll have to wrestle me into submission first."

He'd meant the comment as a joke, but at his words, her eyes darkened and awareness sharpened her features. Tension crackled in the empty room.

So this attraction wasn't all one-sided, he thought with satisfaction. Not that the information meant anything. Stephanie was a single mom with three kids. Which meant she wasn't exactly the kind of woman looking for a good time with no commitment. Too bad.

He might want her, but there was no way he would take advantage of her. He'd grown up with a single mom and he knew how hard that life could be. He wasn't there to contribute to the problem.

He ignored the tension and the need snapping between them and pointed to the bare walls.

"Is this going to be the presidential suite for Serenity House?" he asked.

Stephanie blinked slowly, as if coming out of a trance. "What? Oh. No. It's for me and the kids."

He glanced around at the old gatehouse. It wasn't huge, although there was a second story. "Why would you want to move?"

"It's always been the plan." She rubbed a piece of sandpaper against the door frame, then shook her head and leaned against the wood. "When Marty and I bought the property, we'd intended to fix this place up and move here. That way there would be more rooms to rent out. When he died, my first priority was to get rooms ready for paying guests and this project got put on the back burner. I'm hoping to get it done by midsummer."

"Isn't there more room for you and the kids at the main house?"

"Technically, yes, but when we have a lot of guests, the boys have to be quiet. We're on the third floor with guests underneath. They really try to cooperate, but they're young. Plus I hate reminding them all the time. I don't want their only memories of their childhood to be 'stop making noise.' We're all willing to sacrifice space for privacy."

"Makes sense. Mind if I look around?"

"Help yourself."

He walked through the living room. There was a fireplace at one end, with built-in bookcases on either side. Large windows opened up to the street. The door on the right led to a short hallway and the stairs. There were two bedrooms in back, a bathroom, a kitchen that led to a small dining room, which opened onto the living room. Stephanie stood in that doorway. At the very rear of the house was a utility room with washer and dryer hookups.

Nash climbed the stairs and found a good-size master bedroom with a private bath. The ceilings were high on both floors, and the rooms had big windows, molding and lots of painted wood trim.

He returned to the living room. "Very nice," he said. "Only three bedrooms, though. Will the twins share?"

"They already do and they love it, so that's not a problem."

Nash watched her work for about thirty seconds. When she stretched up past her reach again, the flash of belly skin hit him like a sucker punch.

"Go sand something closer to the floor," he growled and grabbed a piece of sandpaper.

She spun toward him. "What?"

"You're not tall enough. I'll do that."

Her gaze narrowed. "I'm perfectly capable of doing this myself."

"Not without a ladder." He set his hands on her upper arms and gently moved her out of the way. For a brief second he had the impression of curves, heat and feminine scent, then he deliberately turned his back on temptation and went to work on the top of the door frame.

"I can't let you do this," she said.

"Never turn down the offer of free labor. It may not happen again."

"But you're a guest."

"I'm restless and bored. I need something to do."

She laughed. "Right. How silly. Of course I'm the one doing *you* a favor by letting you help me. Why didn't I see that before?"

"Beats me."

He glanced at her over his shoulder. Her chin jutted out and she had her hands on her hips, as if prepared to do battle.

"Just say thank-you and let it go," he told her.

"But I..." She sighed. "Thank you, Nash. I appreciate the help. As long as that's what we call it. Your attempt to guilt me into this by pretending I was doing you a favor was pretty pathetic."

"I've always been told I think fast on my feet."

"I'm a mother of three boys. That makes me a professional in the guilt arena. You're not even close to my league."

He chuckled and returned his attention to the sanding. Under the layers of paint was beautiful old wood, still in great shape.

"Whoever built these houses knew what they were doing," he said. "Good-quality material and great construction."

"Whenever I panic about the mortgage, I remind myself that the B&B will outlast the payments by at least a century. Not that I plan to be around that long."

"The boys will appreciate the inheritance."

"I hope so. If one of them wants to take over the business, that's great. If not, I won't push them. They can sell the house and split the money."

"You're doing some long-term planning."

"I'm a detail person. I try to be responsible. My husband used to tell me I was anal. I guess that comes from being an only child." She knelt on the floor and started sanding the baseboards.

"Not necessarily. I was the responsible one in our family," he said. "As my brother and I are fraternal twins, I can't claim to be the oldest. It's just the way things worked out. I did the right thing and Kevin was a professional screwup. He used to get grounded about three times a week."

Now Nash could smile at the memory, but when it was happening, he used to worry a lot about his brother and how much his mom had to deal with.

"Did he turn out all right?" Stephanie asked.

"Yeah. When we were still in high school, Kevin stole a car. He and his buddies were just joyriding, but the owner pressed charges. It was the last straw for my mom. Kevin was packed off to military school. Apparently the experience scared some sense into him. From there he went to college. After that he became a cop. He joined the U.S. Marshals a few years ago. That's where he is now."

"Talk about a turnaround," she said.

"He's done well." He was pleased by his brother's success, if a little surprised by his sudden engagement.

Nash moved to the dining-room side of the door frame and continued sanding. "Kevin and I had lunch with two of my half brothers today. Travis and Kyle Haynes."

"How did that go?"

"Okay. They filled us in on all the brothers and their families. I don't think we're going to be able to keep everyone straight. They're all married and have kids."

Stephanie rubbed the sandpaper along the baseboard, while Nash tried to keep his attention on his work and off her fanny. With her kneeling like that, her butt stuck up in the air. He was charmed.

"I can't imagine what it would be like to discover a ready-made family," she said and glanced up at him. "What? Am I doing this all wrong?"

"No. You're fine."

"You're looking at me."

He couldn't argue with that. "Want me to work with my eyes closed?"

She rubbed her cheek with her free hand. "Do I look awful?"

"That's not possible."

Her eyes widened and color crept up her face. She ducked her head and began sanding with short, intense strokes. "Great compliment," she murmured. "I wouldn't mind that one stitched on a pillow for my really bad days."

The tension had returned, and with it a longing to do more than just make love. He wanted to touch her and hold her. He wanted to connect.

Where the hell had that thought come from? Nash frowned and returned his attention to his work. No connecting, remember? No relationships. No messy emotions. No disasters.

She cleared her throat. "About your family. There are four brothers and a half sister. At least that's what I've heard. Wait, if she's a half sister, is she still related to you?''

He appreciated the change in subject. ''Apparently. She and the brothers share the same father, as do Kevin and I.''

''I'd heard that Earl Haynes was something of a ladies' man. How did he meet your mother?''

Nash sanded harder. ''She was seventeen and working in a concession stand at the convention center in Dallas. Earl Haynes was in town for a few days. They met, he was charming. Next thing she knew, she was pregnant and he was gone.''

He glanced at Stephanie. She sat back on her heels.

''That's horrible,'' she said.

''Agreed. She'd been raised in a strict home. She didn't know much about men or the world. She tried to get in touch with Earl, but couldn't find him. Her parents made things pretty ugly for her. She gave birth to twins and when she turned eighteen a couple of months later, they threw her out.''

Stephanie sucked in a breath. ''Just like that?''

''Yeah. By then Earl was back in town for his yearly convention. She went looking for him and found him in the arms of another woman. He told my mom that he didn't care about her, and never had. As for his kids, they were her problem.''

He'd been an infant at the time and remembered nothing of what had happened. Yet just thinking about what that bastard had done filled him with fury.

''She ran down to the hotel lobby, crying her heart out,'' Nash continued. ''The woman he'd been with realized she'd made a mistake with Earl, as well. Edie Reynolds took her home to Possum Landing and gave all of us a place to stay while my mom got a job and saved money for an apartment. My brother and I grew up there. It turns out that Edie's two sons were also fathered by Earl Haynes, so Gage is in town, as well, and Quinn, his brother, should be arriving shortly.''

Stephanie shook her head. ''I never could follow soap-opera plot lines, and this is a whole lot more complicated. After moving to Glenwood, I heard a lot about Earl Haynes and his brothers. They were known as local lady-killers. I'd always assumed the talk was just a bunch of rumors, but I guess it was true. What's so interesting is that his sons are terrific men. I guess they used to be pretty wild, but all of them have settled down. You heard about the wives and kids. Brett is in class with one of their boys. I think the twins know a couple of their daughters. There are so many, it's hard to keep them straight. But they're all good kids.''

''They have some crazy notion that Haynes men have boys when they're not in love with the women they're getting pregnant and that they only have girls when they are.''

She laughed. ''Oh, please. That's *so* not possible.''

''Apparently there are plenty of girls to prove the theory. Neither Kevin nor I have kids to put it to the test.''

''I've never heard of such a thing. Of course if it's true, you're going to have to be prepared not to have any boys.'' Her expression turned wistful. ''I really love my sons, but I wouldn't have minded a little girl. Sometimes I miss things like hair ribbons and dresses.''

''It could still happen.''

She grinned. ''Do you see a star parked over my house? There's no way I would ever get married again, so the odds of another child seem slim.''

He felt her words down to his gut. Right up until that moment, he'd been enjoying their conversation, but now he only wanted to walk away. He started sanding again. Slow down, he told himself. Stephanie's reluctance to marry again didn't matter to him. Not one bit.

''You must have loved him very much,'' he said into the silence.

''What? Who?''

''Your husband. You don't want to marry again because you loved him so much.''

She blinked several times, then attacked the baseboards. She used the sandpaper like a scrub brush, then abruptly straightened.

''Look,'' she said. ''There are a lot of reasons I don't want to get married again, but none of them are because I loved Marty too much. I know that sounds horrible, but it's the truth.''

Nash didn't know what to do with the information, nor did he want to understand why the knot in his gut suddenly went away.

There was a moment of awkward silence, then they both spoke at once.

''Go ahead,'' he told her.

Stephanie started sanding again, this time with a little less energy. ''Fertility-gender legend or not, you're going to be an uncle several times over. Brace yourself for the onslaught.''

He hadn't thought of that. ''No wonder the dinner tonight is at a pizza place,'' he said.

She laughed. ''You sound as excited as if you were facing a root canal without anesthetic. Are all the family members expected to be there?''

''Pretty much. Earl is hanging out in Florida with wife number six or seven. He wasn't invited. But all the brothers, kids, half sister and spouses will be there.''

''Sounds like fun.''

Maybe to her. Kevin was engaged, as was Gage. Quinn, the only other single guy in the extended family, had yet to show up. Which meant Nash would be odd man out.

He'd spent his life like that, he reminded himself. It was how he preferred things. But that didn't mean it was going to be comfortable.

''Want to come with me?'' he asked. The invitation was impulsive, but he didn't withdraw it. ''You said the boys know a lot of the Haynes kids. They'd have a good time. You could check out the girls and see if the legend is true.''

Stephanie dropped her piece of sandpaper and wiped her hands on her jeans, all the while considering the invitation. She didn't object to spending some quality time with the featured player in her erotic fantasies, even if she wasn't sure why Nash would want her and the boys along.

''Won't it just be family?'' she asked.

''Too much family. You could protect me.''

He spoke lightly, but she thought she saw something dark and lonely in his eyes.

Get a grip, she told herself. She had to stop reading things into Nash's expression that just weren't there. The man wasn't lonely. He was fine. Most people were fine. The thought of her protecting him was laughable.

"I'll let you have the biggest piece of pizza," he promised.

She had to admit that she was curious about the Haynes family. And a pizza dinner out would thrill the boys. Then there was the issue of being in the same room as Nash—a way she was starting to enjoy spending her time.

She looked at his dark eyes and the way his mouth curved in a half smile. Maybe if she said yes he would accidentally brush his hand against hers. Maybe they would sit close enough together that she could imagine what it would be like to be in bed and all tangled up with him. Not that she needed much help in that department. He was already the star of her intricately detailed daydreams.

What did she have to lose?

"We'd love to join you," she said. "What time do you want us to be ready?"

This was *not* a date, Stephanie told herself that evening as she pulled off her red sweater and grabbed one in teal. It was an evening out at a pizza parlor, so there was no reason for her to sweat what she was wearing. Really.

She pulled on the teal sweater and studied her reflection. The color made her eyes look bluer, but the thicker cable knit made her look as though she didn't have breasts. Complicating the decision of what to wear was the thundering herd of elephants in her stomach and the faint tremor in her fingers.

The latter had caused her to nearly put her eye out while applying mascara.

A knock on the door was followed by Brett calling, "Mom?"

She gave her reflection one last glance and figured this was as good as it was going to get. She fingered her short hair, briefly wished (for the thousandth time in her life) to be tall, then told her oldest to come in.

He pushed open the door and stepped into her room.

"What's up?" she asked as she crossed to the dresser and studied her small earring collection. There were simple gold hoops, a pair of dangling enameled flowers in light pinks and reds and several inexpensive pairs she'd bought on sale. She picked up the gold hoops.

"Why are we going out?" Brett asked.

She glanced up into the mirror and studied her son's reflection. He stood beside her four-poster bed, both arms wrapped around a post, as he swung back and forth. His shoulders were slumped and his expression was solemn.

"Whoa—you're upset because we're going out for *pizza?*" she said as she fastened the first earring. "Are you feeling okay?"

He gave her a half-hearted smile. "The pizza part is fine."

"What about hanging out with your friends and playing video games? Is that what has you bummed?"

The smile broadened. "No."

"Hmm, I don't think it's because we're letting your brothers come along. I know we talked about locking them in the closet when you and I want to leave, but I think it would hurt their feelings. The minivan doesn't have a trunk, so we can't leave them there.''

"Mo-om, I don't want to lock Jason or Adam in a closet."

"Good to know." She finished with the second earring and turned to face him. "That only leaves Nash as the problem."

Brett dropped his gaze and stared at her bedspread. While she would admit that the floral print was very pretty, she didn't think it deserved to be studied with that much intensity.

She walked over to Brett and put her hand on his back. "He's a nice guy. What can I say? He invited us to join him tonight. He's just found out he's related to the Haynes brothers. You know how many of them there are. Plus their wives and their kids." She lowered her voice. "Nash didn't exactly admit this, but I think he wanted us along because he's a little nervous. I think he wants us to be a noisy distraction. That's it."

Brett looked at her. The concern had faded from his eyes. "Yeah?"

"Yeah."

He smiled again. "We're really good at being noisy."

She brushed the hair from his forehead. "I would say you and your brothers are experts."

Nash held open the door to the large pizza restaurant. When Stephanie and the kids had entered, he walked in and saw the small desk up front. The hostess there gave him a big smile. "How many?" she asked.

"We're part of the Haynes party," he said.

"Okay. Through to the back. There are two double doors. You can't miss it. Just follow the noise."

The twins raced ahead with Brett trailing behind them. Nash put his hand on the small of Stephanie's back and urged her forward. As they got closer to the room, the sound of conversation spilled into the main restaurant.

Stephanie leaned close. "Sounds like little more than controlled chaos," she said.

He looked at the dozens of people milling around in the huge room. "I think controlled is stretching it."

They stepped inside where they were greeted by Travis and Kyle. He introduced Stephanie and her kids, then met several wives, two more brothers and three kids.

"This is never going to work," a pretty woman with light brown hair said. "It's only been ten minutes and your eyes are already glazed." She reached into her purse and pulled out a plastic package. "I thought this might happen so I brought name tags."

A petite redhead handed over a box of her own. "Great minds, Elizabeth," she said. "I brought them, too."

The redhead turned to Nash. "I'm Jill, Craig's wife. Craig's the oldest of the brothers." She glanced around the room, then pointed to a tall, dark-haired man with gray at his temples. "Craig's easy to keep track of. He's the best-looking of the brothers."

"He is not," Elizabeth said, then laughed. "I guess we all have our favorites."

"Fortunately that is usually the guy we're married to. Anything else would make these gatherings awkward." Jill looked at Nash, then at Stephanie. "Are we terrifying you? I guess this is really strange. We're such a close-knit family that we don't even think about it, but I remember when I had to meet everyone. It was a little intimidating." She frowned slightly. "Actually it was a lot easier for me back then. Only Travis, Kyle and Austin were married. There weren't as many kids. Did you know that Austin isn't officially a Haynes? It's more of a family member by adoption."

Nash shook his head. "You can't start adding more people," he said. "Not without written permission."

As he spoke he spotted his brother, Kevin, across the room. Haley was next to him, staring at him with a look of love and devotion that made Nash feel he'd accidentally witnessed something personal. He turned away.

"Listen up everybody," Elizabeth said loudly.

A boy of about fourteen stuck two fingers in his mouth and gave a sharp whistle. The room went quiet.

"We have name tags," she continued, waving the box over her head.

"And pens," Jill added.

"Right. Everyone come get a name tag. If you're an adult, put your name first, then a dash and your spouse's name. If you're a child, put your name on top and your parents' names underneath. If you're too young to write, come see me or Jill. Any questions?''

''Is there going to be a quiz?'' Travis asked.

''You bet. And if you fail, you are in big trouble, mister. Don't be messing with me.''

Travis looked pleased at the prospect.

''After you've filled out your name tag,'' Elizabeth continued, ''take a seat at one of the tables. We want to save the big one at the far end for the adults. You kids can sit at the other tables with your friends.''

Jill handed out name tags while Elizabeth passed around several pens. Nash saw Adam and Jason race over to stand with their mother. She talked them through filling out their tags. He waited until they had finished, then wrote his own name. It was only when he glanced around the room that he realized every other tag had either a spouse's name on it or parents' names. Kevin and Haley had put each other's names with theirs on the name tags, as had Gage and Kari.

''Getting ready to bolt?'' Stephanie asked when she'd peeled the back off her tag. ''I'm fairly comfortable in crowds, what with running the B&B and all, but even I'm a little overwhelmed by all this.''

''I'm doing okay,'' he said, taking the tag from her and placing it on her sweater, close to the ribbed neckline. ''I won't pass the quiz, though.''

She grinned. ''I figured if they called on me, I'd cheat by saying everyone was a Haynes. At least then I'd be able to pass with about eight-five-percent accuracy.''

''Good idea.''

His gaze fell onto the tag he'd just pressed into

place and he saw that she didn't have a name after hers either. They were the only two unattached adults at the gathering.

Elizabeth waved them over to take a seat at the large table. Nash found himself seated between Stephanie and Jill. Kevin was on Stephanie's other side.

When everyone was settled, Craig stood. "As the oldest of the Haynes brothers, I would like to thank all of you for coming." He smiled. "We are here tonight to welcome our new brothers." He motioned across the table. "Gage Reynolds, Kevin Harmon and Nash Harmon."

Nash found himself standing, along with Kevin and Gage. There was a round of applause. When they were seated, Craig continued.

"I know we're all anxious to get to know each other. I suggest we start by going around the table and stating our names, where we live and what we do for a living. Oh, and don't forget to introduce your children."

"Yeah, don't forget us," a little dark-haired girl said.

The adults laughed.

"As I already have your attention, I'll start," he said when there was quiet. "I'm Craig Haynes. My beautiful wife, Jill, is sitting right here." He put his hand on her shoulder. "We have five children, the oldest of which is that tall, good-looking eighteen-year-old. Ben was offered a football scholarship at UCLA."

He continued to introduce his five children, then concluded by saying Jill had the hardest job of all—she kept them in line—while he was just a cop.

Travis went next. He rose and introduced his wife, Elizabeth, and their four children. They went around the table. Every single Haynes brother was a cop, until Jordan stood and proclaimed himself as the only Haynes sensible enough to go into fire fighting rather than law enforcement.

Austin Lucas was next. He had the Haynes basics—tall, dark hair and eyes—that distinguished the brothers, but his hair was much longer and he wore a small gold earring. Austin mentioned that he was a Haynes in spirit and heart, rather than by blood.

Gage was next. He talked about his life in Possum Landing, where he was the local sheriff. He introduced his fiancée, and said that his brother, Quinn, should be arriving any day now.

When a tall, dark-haired woman rose, Nash figured she was the half sister he'd heard about. Her introduction confirmed the fact. She explained that her mother, Louise, was home babysitting their latest daughter who had been born only six weeks before.

When it was Nash's turn, he stood. "I'm Nash Harmon. Kevin's twin brother. I'm the smart one."

Everyone laughed.

He grinned when Kevin reached around Stephanie and punched his arm. "I live in Chicago," Nash continued, "where I'm a negotiator for the FBI."

As he added a few more details, he glanced down and saw Stephanie looking at him with surprise. Hadn't he told her what he did for a living?

"I figured there would be more of you than Kevin and I could ever hope to take on on our own," he said lightly, "So I convinced my temporary landlady to take pity on me and help balance the numbers.

This is Stephanie Wynne. Her three boys are…'' He glanced around at the other tables, then spotted Jason and Adam frantically waving. ''Over there.''

He sat down. Craig rose again. Just then several servers entered the room. They had large trays covered with pitchers of root beer, iced tea and beer. When everyone had a drink, Craig raised his glass.

''Welcome,'' he said.

## Chapter Six

Nash lost count of the number of pizzas consumed by the Haynes family. They simply kept on coming. Pitchers of drinks were continually refilled as well. By the time the kids asked to be excused to go play video games and the adults had started moving the chairs around to form small conversational groups, even the servers were looking exhausted.

He'd spent most of dinner talking with Stephanie and Jill, but after the meal, he found himself in the company of his brothers.

*Brothers.* The word still surprised him. How could he and Kevin have been a part of this family for so many years and not have known? How could a man like Earl Haynes get an innocent seventeen-year-old pregnant, abandon her to return to his real family, then produce such honest, sincere, caring offspring?

He crossed to the pitchers of drinks left on the table and poured himself another glass of iced tea. After two beers, he'd switched to the non-alcoholic drink. He wasn't worried about driving, they'd brought Stephanie's minivan and she'd taken the wheel on the way over. Instead he considered the fact that too much beer would make his hostess even more of a temptation than she already was. When sober he found her delightfully intriguing. While drunk he might find her irresistible. Not a good thing for either of them.

He took a drink and surveyed the crowd. He could put a name to the men, but he was still having trouble connecting which spouse belonged with which partner. Hannah was easy. As the only female Haynes, she had many of the physical characteristics of her brothers—she was tall, dark-haired and attractive. Her husband was the only blond male in the room. But after that, things got fuzzy. Was Kyle's wife the average-height brunette with brown eyes or the average-height woman with light brown hair and green eyes?

"Is it making you crazy?"

He turned toward the speaker and found a slender woman standing next to him. Her name tag read "Rebecca—Austin." Underneath were the words "Honorary Haynes through love."

"The guy with the earring," he said.

She smiled. "That would be my husband, yes. He's something of a bad boy."

She spoke the words with a smile and Nash saw the affection twinkling in her eyes.

He glanced over to the man in question and saw him with a young child on his hip. As he spoke with

Travis, Austin absently brought the child's hand to his mouth and blew on the palm. The little boy laughed loudly.

"You seem to have changed his ways," he said.

Rebecca shook her head. "Actually he changed them all on his own. He was always the quiet rebel, but he's mellowed."

Austin looked content, Nash thought. He was a man comfortable and at peace with his world. Two things Nash rarely experienced.

He turned his attention back to the woman in front of him. She was lovely, with classically beautiful features that spoke of a gentler time. Unlike the other wives who were dressed in slacks and blouses, Rebecca wore a long dress edged in lace. Her dark, curly hair came to the middle of her back. She reminded him of a character in one of those British period movies—the kind that made him head directly for ESPN if he ever turned the television to one by accident.

"Are you overwhelmed?" she asked. "It's a huge family."

"I'm getting the adults," he said. "The kids are going to take longer."

"We all have trouble with that. At one time or another, each of us has had to stop one of the children and ask who they belong to."

She took a step closer and lowered her voice. "When Travis told us that there were long-lost Hayneses around, everyone was thrilled. When I heard you were all single, I was doubly delighted."

He raised his eyebrows. There was no way she was asking for herself.

She laughed. "I have a friend. D.J. doesn't know

it yet, but she's ready to settle down. I was planning on fixing her up with one of you. The thing is, you're not all single, are you?''

"Gage and Kevin have had a change in circumstance in the past few months.''

"So I heard.'' She grinned. "I had high hopes for you, Nash, but they've recently been dashed.''

She turned and nodded across the room. He followed her gaze and saw Stephanie talking with Jill.

As Stephanie spoke, she moved her hands. A smile tugged at the corners of her mouth. Jill responded and they both laughed. He was standing too far away to hear the sound, but he imagined it and smiled in return.

"Oh, my,'' Rebecca said. "It's worse than I thought.''

"It's not anything.''

"Really?''

"Yes.'' He wasn't about to tell her about his no-relationships rule. "I'm only in town for a couple of weeks.''

"Sometimes plans change.''

"Not mine.''

"Too bad.'' She shrugged. "But if you're leaving that quickly, you wouldn't be right for D.J. even if you were available. Which leaves the mysterious Quinn Reynolds. Maybe I can fix them up.''

Nash considered the idea. On the surface Quinn was a charmer, with plenty of stories and a woman on each arm. But underneath…he wasn't like the rest of them. Quinn lived in a world that would break most men. He did things, saw things, no human should endure.

"Quinn's a great guy," he said. "But more than a little dangerous."

Rebecca looked intrigued. "D.J. enjoys a challenge."

"Quinn would be that. But he's a loner. Women tend to have one purpose in his life, and it's not cooking."

He'd expected Rebecca to be shocked, but instead she grinned. "How fun. That would make D.J. completely crazy."

Nash wouldn't have used that word to describe Quinn's relationships with his women, but then he didn't know this D.J. person, either.

"You want to torture your friend?" he asked.

"No, but I can't figure out another way to get her happily married."

"Okay, then." Nash took a step back. Sometimes women completely confused him.

Rebecca excused herself. As she walked away, Stephanie joined Nash. She glanced at her watch.

"Would you mind if we collected the boys and left? It's a school night and they're already wired enough from school getting out in a couple of days. If I have any prayer of a decent bedtime for them, I need to get moving now."

"Sure. Want me to help?"

"Please. Why don't you look for the twins? They'll be together and more cooperative. I'll pull the car up front and get Brett."

They said goodbye to the Haynes family, then walked into the main restaurant. The video-game room was by the door. Nash spotted Jason and Adam on a bench by the wall. Adam stood as he approached, but Jason only blinked sleepily.

"Time to head home," Nash said.

"I'm ready," Adam said.

Jason rose, then held out his arms. "I'm tired."

Nash stared at him. A small child holding up his arms was a pretty universal symbol. Even living a child-free existence, Nash got it right away. Jason wanted to be carried.

Nash hesitated. It wasn't because he thought Jason would be too heavy or that Stephanie would mind. Instead he paused because something inside of him warned him that this was potentially problematic. He didn't do relationships—not with women, not with friends, not with kids. Relationships required a level of letting go he didn't permit himself. Control was all that stood between him and chaos.

Jason's implied trust made him uneasy. He'd only known the kids a couple of days. So why was Jason so comfortable around Nash?

"He wants to be carried," Adam said, as if he thought Nash didn't get it.

"I know."

There didn't seem to be a graceful way out of the situation and Nash didn't want to make a scene over nothing. So he bent forward and pulled the boy up toward his chest. Jason instantly closed his arms around Nash's neck and rested his head on his shoulder. His small legs wrapped around Nash's waist.

Nash put one arm around the boy to hold him in place, then motioned for Adam to lead the way. Instead the eight-year-old tucked his fingers into Nash's free hand and leaned close.

"Is Mommy bringing the car around?" he asked sleepily.

"Yes. Come on."

He led the way to the front of the restaurant, then out into the night. Brett was already waiting on the sidewalk. He took one look at the three of them, then turned away. But not before Nash saw the hostility flare in his eyes.

The brief glimpse of the twelve-year-old's raw hurt and anger stirred something familiar in Nash.

Stephanie drove up and broke his concentration. Then he got caught up in settling the twins. As he was about to climb into the passenger seat, Kevin stepped out of the restaurant.

"What did you think?" his brother asked.

Nash looked back at the pizza place. "Good people."

"I agree." Kevin grinned and slapped him on the back. "See you soon." He ducked his head into the minivan. "Nice to meet you, Stephanie. If this guy gives you any trouble, you let me know."

She smiled. "So far he's been terrific, but if that changes, I'll call."

"You do that. Night."

Kevin stepped back into the restaurant. Stephanie watched him go.

"You have a great family," she said. "You're lucky."

Nash had never thought of himself that way, but in this case, maybe she was right.

Stephanie sucked in a breath and did her best to hold on to her temper. "Brett, it's late, it's a school night and you're behaving like a brat. If you're trying to convince me that you're not mature enough to handle evenings out on a weeknight, you're doing a great job.''

Her oldest flopped back on the bed and stared at the ceiling. Since arriving back from their dinner out with Nash and his family, Brett had been sullen, uncommunicative and mouthy. She couldn't figure out what the problem was. Sure he was inching closer to being a teenager, but hormones couldn't kick in over the course of a couple of hours, could they?

She sank onto the bed and put her hand on his stomach. ''I know you had a good time. I saw you laughing.''

''It was okay.''

''Just okay? I thought you were having more fun than that.''

He shrugged.

She began to rub his stomach, something she'd done when he was little and not feeling well. ''I'm not leaving until you tell me what has your panties in a bunch. I'm just going to sit right here. After a while, I might start singing.''

He continued to stare at the ceiling, but she saw his mouth twitch. All the boys thought she had a horrible voice and begged her not to sing. Plus, he would really hate the panty remark. She wondered which one would get to him first.

''I don't wear panties.''

''I do the laundry. I already know that.'' She leaned over him. ''How about I just stare at you?''

She made her eyes as wide as possible and forced herself not to blink. Brett pressed his lips together, but it was too late. First he smiled, then he grinned, then he giggled and turned away.

"Stop staring at me!"

She relaxed her face and sat back. "I will if you'll talk."

He turned on his side so he was facing her, but instead of looking at her face, he studied the blanket. "Do you still love Dad?"

She was unprepared for the question. Brett didn't want to have this talk very often, but whenever he did, she felt uncomfortable. She always went for the easy answer, rather than the truth, because that's what Brett wanted to hear. Because she wanted her son to remember his father as a good person and his parents as happy together.

"Of course I still love him," she said gently. "Why do you ask?"

He shrugged.

"Is this about Nash? Are you worried that something's going on between us?"

Another shrug.

"He's being nice," she said. "I like him, but that doesn't mean anything. He's on vacation. When his vacation is over, he's going back to Chicago."

Where the handsome widower probably had dozens of elegant, sophisticated women vying for his attention. Where he wouldn't even remember a single mom with three kids who had an embarrassing crush on him.

"Do you want to, like, you know, go out with him?"

Honestly she would much prefer to stay in with Nash, but that wasn't what Brett wanted to know. Two weeks ago she would have told her son that she never planned on dating or getting involved with a man ever. But Nash's arrival had shown her that there were some empty places in her life. While she would never be stupid enough to risk marriage, she wouldn't mind a little male companionship now and then.

"I can't imagine Nash and me on date," she said truthfully. "But your dad has been gone three years. While my feelings for him haven't changed, there will come a time when I want to start dating again."

Brett's blue eyes filled with tears. "Why? Why can't you just love Dad?"

"Because he's gone." She pulled him into a sitting position, then drew him into her arms. "When you get a little older, you're going to think girls are a whole lot better than icky. I promise. So you're going to go out. You may even have a girlfriend."

He writhed in her arms. "Mo-om."

"Just listen. So you have this girl you really care about. Will you still love your brothers?"

He looked at her. "What does that have to do with anything?"

"Just answer the question. Will you still love them?"

"I guess. If they're not being dopey."

"Will you still love me?"

"Sure."

"That's my point. The human heart has the capacity to love as many people as we want to let into our lives. If I start dating or not, nothing about my feelings for you, the twins or even Dad are going to change. There's more than enough room for everyone."

"But I like thinking about you with Dad."

"You can keep thinking about that. I didn't leave him, honey. He died. We mourned him and we still love him. That's the right thing to do. But it's also right to live our lives and be happy. Don't you think your dad would have wanted that for all of us?"

Stephanie knew that Marty would have loved the idea of being mourned endlessly by his wife and children, but she wasn't about to lay that guilt on her twelve-year-old.

Brett nodded slowly. "But you're not going out with Nash."

"I'm not."

"Promise?"

"Nash and I will not go out of this house on a date." She made an X over her heart. "But that's as much as my life as you get to dictate, young man. And should I decide to go out with someone, you're going to have to accept the idea. Agreed?"

"Yeah. No problem."

"Good."

She kissed his forehead, then released him. After he scrambled under the covers, she tucked them in around him, said good-night and walked out into the hallway. After closing the door, she moved down the stairs.

She wondered when Brett had started to consider Nash a threat. Was there something in his behavior, or was her son able to subconsciously pick up on her strong attraction? Not that it mattered. She'd been very comfortable agreeing to no dates with Nash. Somehow she couldn't see him offering to take her to dinner and a movie. He wasn't a "dinner and a movie" kind of guy. Nash was more late-night walks along the river and hot, passionate kisses up against the crumbling stone wall of the ancient castle.

Stephanie smiled. At least he was in *her* imagination. As there was neither a river nor a castle nearby, she was probably safe. Not that she wanted to be.

She reached the main floor and turned toward the kitchen, then stopped when a slight movement caught her attention. As she spun around, she saw Nash pacing restlessly across the living-room rug. He glanced up and saw her, came to a stop and shrugged.

"I'm a little wound from the dinner," he said. "I'm not ready to go up to bed. Am I bothering you?"

Not in the way he meant. "Of course not. I have to make cookies for the twins to take to school tomorrow. There are few things less interesting than watching someone bake. You want to come into the kitchen and be bored for a while? It will probably help you sleep."

"Sure."

As soon as he agreed, she wanted to stop and bang her head against a nearby wall. Watching her might be boring for him, but having him near was wildly exciting for her. She really didn't need to spend more time with him. Hanging around with Nash only seemed to encourage her overactive imagination. Before their dinner tonight she'd thought he was sexy and roguishly charming. After their dinner, she was starting to like him.

She'd enjoyed watching him interact with his family. He'd been caring and understanding with the dozens of kids running around, attentive and interested in his brothers. She'd been stunned to find out what he did for a living. So much for her theory that he was a professor or sold shoes. Instead he inhabited a dark and dangerous world, which only made him more physically appealing.

Stephanie told herself that she had to stop imagining Nash as the bare-chested caveman whisking her off into the wilderness. The poor guy had signed on to be her guest, not the star of her erotic fantasies. If he knew what she was thinking, he would be forced to run screaming into the night.

She collected ingredients for chocolate chip cookies and set them on the counter. Nash took a seat at the kitchen table, then half rose.

"Can I help?"

She shook her head. "I've done this so many times, I don't have to look at a recipe. But if you behave, I'll let you have a sample fresh from the oven."

"Deal."

She grabbed a couple of eggs and put them next to the canister of flour. "So what did you think of tonight?" she asked.

"It went well. I'm not sure I can keep everyone straight."

"I wouldn't want to try," she admitted. "The name tags were a great idea." She measured brown sugar. "Where in Chicago do you live?"

"I have a condo by the lake. I can walk to a lot of great restaurants. There's a good jogging trail nearby."

"I've never been, but I can't imagine you do much jogging in the winter."

"True. Then I hit the gym."

And he had the body to prove it. Although she doubted Nash worked out to be buff. No doubt it was required for his job. She tried not to sigh at the image of him in a ratty T-shirt and shorts, lifting heavy weights. Instead she channeled her energy into vigorously whipping her eggs.

"I grew up with one brother and my mom," he said quietly. "I've never had any experience with a large family."

"The Hayneses will take some getting used to," she said. "But they'll be worth the effort."

He nodded. "What about you? Are you one of seven?"

"Not exactly." She opened the bottle of vanilla and picked up her measuring spoons. "I was an only child. My parents were artists. Very focused on their work and each other." She gave him a slight smile. "They didn't believe in paying attention to the outside world. Things like electric bills and empty kitchen cupboards didn't faze them. I grew up pretty quickly. Someone had to be the responsible one and it turned out to be me."

His dark gaze settled on her face. "Was that tough?"

"Sometimes." When she wanted to be a kid, like her friends. "But I learned a lot, too. I was really prepared for the real world when I left for college."

"Did you want a big family?"

"Sure. While I was growing up, I thought it would be terrific. I had it all planned, from my husband to our five kids to our assortment of dogs, cats and small rodents."

She'd thought the same when she'd married Marty. But by the time she'd figured out she'd made a horrible mistake and discovered she was pregnant in the same week, her plans had changed. She'd resigned herself to having one child. The twins had been an accident. A blessing, but an unplanned one.

If only, she thought. If only Marty had been more willing to be a grown-up instead of an overgrown child. If only she'd seen the truth earlier. Except then she wouldn't have her boys, and she loved them more than anything.

"Stephanie?"

"Huh?" She glanced up and saw him watching her.

"Are you all right? You got pretty quiet."

"Sorry. Just thinking."

He rose and crossed to the island. "About your late husband?"

"Yes, but not in the way you think." She didn't want Nash to worry that he'd made her miss Marty.

"Was it being out with me? The whole 'meet the family' circus?"

"No. That was great. I really enjoyed tonight." She tried to smile, but he was standing only a couple of feet of counter space away and his intense, dark stare took her breath away. She cleared her throat. "I don't get out that much."

"With three boys and your own business, you probably don't have time to date much."

"Date?" She laughed. "Like that ever happens."

"Why doesn't it?"

"Good question."

She dumped the dry ingredients into the batter and began to stir. As the mixture thickened, she had to really push to get the wooden spoon through.

"I'll do that," he said, stepping around the island and moving next to her.

Before she realized what was happening, he'd taken the spoon from her and was making quick work of the mixing. She blinked in surprise.

"Why do you do that?" she asked. "Why are you always so happy to help?"

"Why not?"

She didn't have an answer she was willing to share. Telling him she'd long ago learned not to depend on anyone made her sound pathetic.

"Do these go in next?" he asked, nodding toward the open bag of chocolate chips.

"Yes." She dumped the chips into the batter.

"So why don't you date?"

She stared at the swirling mixture, rather than risk looking at him. Dangerous, dangerous question. "I just…there aren't many men interested and I don't seem to meet any."

"Interested men?"

"Any men."

"So it's not that *you're* not interested."

"I—" The questions were going from bad to worse. Interested? Was she? Not in love. She'd learned that lesson in spades. But in a good man? Someone who would be fun and funny and caring? Someone who would hold her and ease the trembling ache deep inside?

"I could be interested," she admitted softly.

"Good."

He dropped the wooden spoon into the bowl and turned toward her. Before she realized what was happening, before she could catch her breath or even consider if this was as crazy as it seemed, he'd pulled her into his arms. Just like that. She was pressed up against his hard, masculine body and then his face was getting closer and she knew he was going to kiss her.

Stephanie's last rational thought was that it had been twelve years since a man other than Marty had kissed her and that there was a more than even chance she'd completely forgotten what to do.

Then Nash claimed her mouth in a warm, tender, erotic kiss that made her heart freeze in midbeat and her brain completely shut down. There wasn't any thinking, there was only feeling. Feeling and doing.

He pressed his lips against hers with just enough pressure to make her want more. Strong, large hands settled on her back. She felt his fingers, the heat of his palms, the brush of his thighs against her own. His scent surrounded her, enticed her, made her legs weak and her muscles slack. She had to wrap her arms around his neck to stay standing.

Then his mouth moved against her. Slowly, discovering, teasing. He brushed his tongue against her lower lip. She had no will and parted instantly. Excitement raced through her. The sound of her breathing filled her head. She wanted with a desperation that should have terrified her, but instead only made her reckless. She wanted deep, hot kisses and wild abandon. She wanted his hands everywhere. She wanted to touch and to be touched, to be wet, to be filled. She wanted to lose herself in an orgasm that would shake the very fabric of the space-time continuum.

So when he again swept his tongue against the inside of her lower lip, she moaned low in her throat.

When he moved inside and brushed against her, letting her taste him, feel him, dance with him, she respond with an intensity that was as foreign to her as the fiery need spiraling through her.

She kissed him deeply, matching each thrusting stroke with one of her own. When he moved his hands from her back to her rear, she arched against him, flattening her belly against an impressive hardness.

They both strained to get closer and closer still. Heads tilting, tongues mating, hands roving, they gasped and kissed and nipped and surged.

She traced the length of his spine, then felt his high, tight rear end. As her fingers dug into his flesh, his arousal flexed against her stomach. He slipped his hands to her hips, then to her waist. At the same time, he pulled away from her mouth and instead began to kiss her jaw, her neck, then that sweet spot right below her ear. He licked the sensitive skin and while she was still caught up in the pleasure, he sucked on her ear lobe. At the same moment, his hands closed over her sensitized breasts.

She had to bite her lip to keep from screaming. Long fingers cupped her curves, while his thumbs and forefingers caressed her hard, aching nipples. Need raced through her. Need and desire and longing for more. She wanted to tear off her clothes, and his. She wanted him to take her right there, on the counter. She wanted it hard and fast, her legs spread, him buried deep, thrusting and thrusting until they both lost control in a shuddering release.

"Nash," she breathed and reached for the buttons on his shirt.

He grabbed the hem of her sweater and started to

tug. Right then, there was a loud creak from overhead.

Stephanie knew it was just the old house settling as the night temperature dropped, but it was enough to remind her of the fact that they really *were* in her kitchen and that she had three children sleeping upstairs. She stiffened slightly. Nash read the signal for what it was and immediately stepped back.

His face was flushed, his eyes dilated, his mouth damp from their kisses. He looked like a man more than ready for a walk on the wild side. She had a feeling she looked just as...aroused.

Just don't think about how long it's been since you had sex, she told herself. The reality would be too depressing for words.

In the silence of the kitchen, their breathing sounded loud and unnaturally fast. Nash recovered enough to speak first. Or maybe he wasn't as nervous as she was.

"I haven't kissed anyone in a while," he said, his voice thick with passion and slightly wry. "I don't remember it being like that."

She had to clear her throat before speaking. "Me, neither."

"You okay?"

She nodded.

"Want me to apologize?" he asked.

"No. Not unless you're sorry." Oh, please, not that. She couldn't stand that.

His dark eyes crinkled at the corners as he smiled. "Not even close."

He raised his hand toward her, then dropped it back to his side. "I'd better head upstairs before... Well, before we start at it again."

She didn't want him to go, but she knew it was for the best. Ah, maturity. Why was it never as much fun as acting like an irresponsible kid?

"Sleep well," he said as he turned to leave.

"Unlikely," she said before she could stop herself.

He glanced at her and grinned. "Tell me about it."

## Chapter Seven

Stephanie thought about looking at the clock, but the first time she'd checked it had been about ten to four in the morning. She doubted it was much past four now. Although she'd managed to doze on and off for a few hours, she'd spent most of the night alternating between reliving the incredible kiss she and Nash had shared and pulling the pillow over her face to muffle her shrieks of embarrassment.

What had she been thinking? *Had* she been thinking?

No, she told herself. She hadn't been thinking at all. She'd been reacting. She'd been feeling and touching and wanting. Not thinking.

If she'd taken the time to consider her actions, she never would have allowed herself to respond with such wanton abandon. She'd been crazed with passion—a new experience for her. Her feelings of need had spiraled out of control in less than ten seconds of first contact. What did that say about her?

Stephanie didn't have an answer. In all the years she and Marty had been married she'd never felt so needy. So alive. So desperate.

"Desperate?" she murmured into the night.

She didn't like the sound of that. It made her think of pitiful people doing inappropriate things without considering the consequences.

Oh, like wanting to do it right there on the counter, next to the batch of cookie batter?

She pulled the pillow over her face and groaned.

She wasn't desperate, she told herself forcefully. If she was desperate, she would be out eyeing all the single fathers in town. She'd met a few at school events. A couple had even asked her out. While she'd appreciated the invitations, nothing about them had sent her into sexual spasms the way Nash did. She'd thought they were nice, pleasant men who didn't tempt her in the least. She'd found it tragically simple to remember that she absolutely didn't want to get involved again because a relationship with a man meant taking on more responsibility. Thanks but no thanks.

With Nash it was different. She found it far too easy to forget her rules and instead focus on how the man looked as he walked through a room. She could spend an embarrassing amount of time thinking about his mouth, his voice, his hands. And all that was *before* he'd kissed her. Now that she had actual evidence of the potential, she could easily spend the better part of her day considering the sexual possibilities. They could—

Stephanie sat up in bed and clicked on the lamp on her nightstand.

"Snap out of it," she whispered aloud. "You're a mature, responsible woman with a successful business and three kids. You have more guests arriving in a few days, summer vacation starting at the end of the week and laundry multiplying like rabbits. You simply cannot waste your days thinking about making love with Nash Harmon. It's not right. It's not healthy. It's not likely to happen."

The last was the most tragic, she thought as she flung herself back on the bed. If only he would creep into her room in the dead of night and take advantage of her. If only he would—

She sat up again, but this time it wasn't to give herself a stern but useless talking-to. Instead her mouth dropped open as a horrifying thought occurred to her.

She and Nash had kissed. Right there in her kitchen. It had been painfully real and erotic and incredible and wow. But she didn't know why he'd done it or if he was going to regret it come morning. Regardless, she was going to have to face him and act as if nothing had happened. She was going to have to pretend not to be affected by his presence or his voice, and she was going to have to act that way in front of her children.

She moaned, then rolled onto her side and hugged the pillow close. Why hadn't she thought that part through before she'd allowed herself to come unglued in his arms? What if *he* was having seconds thoughts? What if he thought she was some sex-starved freak and all he wanted was to pack his bags and move out? What if he was laughing at her?

Each thought was more awful than the one before. Stephanie endured the potentials for humiliation for as long as she could, then gave up and threw back the covers. She wasn't going to lie here for another couple of hours, looking for trouble. With her luck, it would come looking for her, regardless of her opinion on the matter. Better to face the day with a smile and a happy heart.

She crossed to her bathroom and clicked on the light. It was worse than she thought. In addition to spiky hair and pale skin, she had bags the size of carry-on luggage under her eyes. Scratch that starting-the-day-with-a-smile stuff. She was going to have spend the next hour with a cold compress under her eyes.

Nash heard footsteps on the stairs shortly after five that morning. He figured it was probably Stephanie getting an early start to her day. While he wanted to get up and join her in whatever she might have planned, he didn't think she would appreciate the interruption.

Instead he continued to sit in the tufted chair in front of the window and stare out at the faint hint of light on the eastern horizon.

He felt good. Hell of a thing to admit, but it was true. Life coursed through his body. Desire rumbled just below the surface and threatened to surge back into existence at any moment. Interest prickled at the edges of his mind. He no longer wanted to get lost in his job—instead he was making plans, anticipating.

When had that happened? It wasn't all about the kiss and his reawakened sexual need. Oh, sure, he wanted Stephanie. All she had to do was name the time and place and he would be there. But this feeling inside was about something more.

Was it finding out about his family? Was it a combination of things? Was it that he'd finally be forced to look up from his work long enough to remember there was a world out here? Did it matter?

As he stared out the window, he had a sudden flashback to what she'd felt like in his arms. How her body had yielded to his. Curves to hard planes. She'd smelled so damn good. His fingers flexed as he recalled the feel of her breasts and how she'd moaned when he'd brushed against her tight nipples.

His body reacted quickly and predictably. Nash chuckled as blood sprinted to his groin. The ache there thickened until it bordered on uncomfortable, but that was okay with him. Feeling all of this beat feeling nothing, and he'd been feeling nothing for a long time.

Since well before Tina's death.

He closed his eyes against the growing light. He didn't want to think about her. Not today. He didn't want to live in the past or wonder what he could have done differently. He just wanted to be.

Life beckoned. He heard the call, felt the stirring inside himself. Was he going to answer? Was it safe?

He opened his eyes and considered the question. There were no guarantees. He'd always known, but Tina's death had reminded him in an ugly way. Joining the rest of the world would mean taking risks. He could never forget that he had to stay in control. He couldn't risk letting that go, not even for a second.

His cell phone rang. Nash grabbed it from the desk by the window and glanced at the display screen. He recognized the number and punched the Talk button.

"Harmon."

"Tell me you're on a beach somewhere enjoying the sun."

Nash grinned. "Jack, it's a little after five in the morning on the west coast. There isn't any sun."

His boss swore. "Sorry. I always forget about the time difference. Did I wake you?"

"No. I was up."

"Want to tell me why?"

Nash thought about Stephanie and what they'd done the previous evening. "Not a chance."

"Huh. I can't decide if your being cryptic is good or bad."

"I can't help you there."

"You mean you won't. Never mind. I'm not calling to mess with you too much. I thought I'd bring you up to date on what's going on around the office."

"Right." Nash grinned. "You're calling to check up on me. Why don't you admit it?"

"Because I don't have to. Marie's pregnant."

Nash's grin broadened. "Don't sound so broken up about it."

"She already has eight or nine kids. Why does she want another one? What if she doesn't come back? She keeps my life running smoothly. I don't want to have to train some other assistant."

"Hold on. I want to pause a moment and feel the compassion."

Jack swore again. "I know, I know. I should be happy for her."

"You would be if it weren't so inconvenient for you."

"Right."

Nash shook his head. "For one thing, Marie only has two children, not eight or nine. For another, she loves her job more than most of us do. She's not going to quit."

"That's what she says, but I don't believe her."

"That's your problem."

Jack called him a name, then brought him up to date on several projects. "So how are you feeling?" he asked when he was done.

"I felt fine before I left and I still feel fine," Nash said.

"You know what I mean. I worry about you. Too many hours, no time off. Hell, Nash, you don't even call in sick."

"That's because I don't get sick."

"You work late, you work holidays. It's not natural. I don't want you burning out. I need you at the top of your game."

"So your concern is all about you."

"Damn straight." Jack was quiet for a second. "You need to talk to somebody."

Nash's chest tightened. "I did."

"You had the required sessions with an in-house psychologist, because I threatened to fire you if you didn't. I'm talking about someone outside the bureau. Tina's death was a shock to all of us. Violence leaves a scar."

The conversation was a variation of one they'd

had a dozen times before. "I've dealt with it in my own way."

"That's what scares me. Do you still blame yourself?"

Nash knew the right answer. He was supposed to say that he didn't. That it was just one of those things. Instead he told the truth.

"I should have known. I should have done something."

"You're good, but you're not that good. No one is."

But Nash knew he was supposed to be. He was supposed to be one of the best.

"So you're having fun?" Jack asked in a change of subject.

Nash thought about what he'd been doing for the past few days. "Yeah. I am."

"Good to hear. Take it easy. Relax. Become one of the living again."

"I'm working on it."

"I wish I could believe that. You need to get laid."

Nash chuckled. "Funny you should mention that. I was just thinking the same thing myself."

"For real?"

"Yup."

"That's the best news I heard all day. Good for you."

"Don't be so enthusiastic," Nash said. "You're starting to worry me."

Jack laughed. "Fair enough. Okay, you go find a good-looking broad and I'll hold things together here. See you in a couple of weeks."

"Sure thing. Bye."

Nash pushed the End button on his cell, then tossed the phone back onto the desk. Jack was old school, and the least politically correct guy Nash knew. But he was a good man who genuinely cared. He wanted Nash to let the past go—not just for the sake of his team, but for Nash himself.

Nash wasn't ready to let anything go, not yet, but he was willing to take his friend's advice about finding a "good-looking broad." He already had one in mind.

Nash showered and dressed, but waited until close to seven before going downstairs. After what had happened the previous night, he wasn't sure what to expect. At the bottom of the stairs he saw that the kitchen door was closed and the dining room door was open. Taking that as a hint, he crossed to the dining room and found his usual place for one already set. The local paper, along with *USA TODAY,* sat to the left of his napkin and flatware. A basket of still-warm scones sat next to an empty coffee cup. Before he could check the carafe, the door to the kitchen pushed open and Stephanie entered.

She had returned to her B&B-owner uniform of tailored slacks, low-heeled pumps and a sweater that clung to her upper body in such a way as to interfere with his brain waves. Makeup accentuated her blue eyes…eyes that were not looking directly at him.

"Good morning," she said politely as she carried a full coffeepot over to the table. She unscrewed the lid of the carafe, then filled it with the steaming liquid.

"What would you like in your omelette?" she asked. "I have several cheeses, an assortment of vegetables, bacon, ham and sausage. Or you could have the meat on the side.''

She offered him a friendly smile that didn't chase away the air of nervousness.

So she'd decided to go the "all business" route to deal with whatever morning-after jitters she might be having. Nash could have wished for something else, but he understood her decision. She didn't know him from a rock. She was a woman with responsibilities and they didn't include playing footsie with the paying guests.

"An omelette would be great," he said. "Cheddar cheese and whatever vegetables you have around. I would appreciate a side of bacon, as well."

"No problem. It will be about fifteen or twenty minutes. The boys are due down any second and I want to get them fed. Is that all right?"

"Of course."

She nodded and left, all without ever looking directly at him. Nash took his seat and opened the paper, but he didn't actually see the print.

Was she having second thoughts about last night? Did she regret the kiss? When they'd parted, he would have bet she'd been as pleasantly surprised and turned on as he had been. But after several hours to reflect, she could have decided it had all been a mistake.

He didn't want her to think that. He wanted her to want him as much as he wanted her.

Nash shook his head. Okay—he had it bad. He was on the verge of behaving like an idiot over a woman and he couldn't remember the last time that had happened.

The sound of feet clattering on the stairs caught

his attention. The boys were arguing over whose turn it was to pick up in the family room upstairs. Apparently they all tried to get in the kitchen door at once because there were shouts of "Stop pushing me," and "Get out of my way!"

Nash smiled as he imagined the three of them shoving and laughing and then bursting into the kitchen. He heard Stephanie's warm greeting, then the sound of chairs being pulled out.

For the first time in years, he found himself not wanting to be by himself. As he sat alone in the dining room, he listened to murmurs of conversation and explosions of laughter, all the while wishing he could be a part of it. Then, without considering the consequences of his actions, he picked up his carafe of coffee, his cup and the basket of scones, then walked into the kitchen.

Once again, conversation ceased. He could feel the boys looking at him, but his attention centered on Stephanie. She had just set a carton of eggs onto the center island. Her head snapped up and her mouth parted slightly. Color crept up her cheeks.

"The dining room was a little empty this morning," he said by way of explanation. "Would you mind if I joined you in here?"

Emotions raced across her face, but they went too quickly for him to read them. If she hesitated for too long, or looked too uncomfortable, he was going to head back to the dining room and keep out of her way for the rest of his stay.

The corners of her mouth turned up slightly and her blush deepened. When she finally met his gaze, he saw a heat flaring in her eyes that matched the one raging inside him.

"That would be nice," she said.

The twins shifted their chairs to make room for him between them. He set his coffee and scones down on the table and collected an empty chair. When he was seated he saw that Brett didn't look as happy to see him as everyone else did.

Before he could think of something to say to the preteen, Jason flipped back the napkin on the basket and peered inside.

"Whatcha got?" he asked, then wrinkled his nose.

"Don't you like scones?"

Jason shook his head. "They taste funny."

Nash offered one to Adam, who shrunk back in his chair as if he'd been offered bug guts. Nash glanced at Brett and raised his eyebrows.

Brett reached across the table and took one. "They're still kids," he said as he set the scone next to his toast. "They don't like these yet."

"Makes sense," Nash said, trying not to smile. The way Brett talked, he was pushing forty instead of barely turned twelve.

Nash poured himself a cup of coffee. Behind him, Stephanie cracked eggs into a frying pan.

"There's a talent show today," Jason announced. "At school. A girl in my class is going to dance ballet." He wrinkled his nose. "She's got this funny-looking skirt thing. A tutu. It sticks out and is all stiff. But if you throw it across the room it goes really far."

"A boy in my class plays the drums," Adam said from Nash's other side. "And three girls are going to sing a song from the radio."

"Sounds like fun."

Adam nodded.

The twins chatted all through breakfast. Brett didn't say much, but he kept his eye on Nash. Stephanie slid their scrambled eggs onto their plates, then whipped up Nash's omelette. While he finished eating, the boys stood and began collecting their backpacks. There was a flurry of activity as each child received a hug, a kiss and lunch money.

"Have a good day," Stephanie said as she tucked change into Adam's backpack and closed the small zippered compartment. "I love you."

She gave them each another quick hug, although Brett ducked out of her embrace. Then the boys thundered to the front of the house and outside. The door slammed behind them.

Nash finished his breakfast and poured himself another cup of coffee. Stephanie pushed open the door to the dining room and watched out the front window until they were all on the bus.

As she stood there, he remembered his own mornings as a child. His mother had always made sure she was there to fix them breakfast and pack their lunches. Then she'd walked them out of the house. The last thing she'd said every school morning through to his high-school graduation had been that she loved them each more than she could say and that they were the best part of her world.

For a while, he had stopped believing her on both counts. Now, looking back with the hindsight of an adult, he knew that nothing had changed on her part.

Stephanie returned to the kitchen where she fussed with dishes, munched on an extra piece of bacon and fluttered nervously until Nash used his foot to push out the chair across from his.

"Have a seat," he said.

She glanced from him to the chair, then sighed. "Okay. I guess we need to talk about it."

She poured herself a cup of coffee and joined him at the table.

She looked at him, then away. Color climbed high on her cheeks, retreated, then returned. Nash figured it was all up to him.

He decided to start with something easy. "Was my joining you and the boys for breakfast a problem?"

"What?" She'd been tracing a pattern on the table. Now she raised her head and stared at him. "No. Of course not." She smiled. "I thought it was nice. If you want to plan on joining us for the rest of your stay, I'll just set an extra place in here, rather than the dining room. It's not a problem at all."

He'd half expected her to ask him why. Why did he want to join them? Not that he had an answer. On some level he knew that being around her and her kids allowed him to forget. Without work to distract him, there was too much time to think. But that was only one of the reasons. The others all had something to do with him enjoying her and the boys' company.

"I'd like that," he said. "So if that's not the issue, what is? Last night?"

She swallowed, then nodded slowly. "*Issue* isn't exactly the word I'd use. I thought..." She looked away. "You're so calm."

"And you're not?"

"Isn't it obvious?" She clutched her coffee cup in both hands. "I just... I guess what I really want to know is why it happened."

# GET FREE BOOKS and a FREE GIFT WHEN YOU PLAY THE...

## Lucky 7

### SLOT MACHINE GAME!

*Just scratch off the silver box with a coin. Then check below to see the gifts you get!*

## YES!
I have scratched off the silver box. Please send me the 2 free Silhouette Special Edition® books and gift for which I qualify. I understand I am under no obligation to purchase any books, as explained on the back of this card.

**335 SDL DRRG**                    **235 SDL DRRW**

| | |
|---|---|
| FIRST NAME | LAST NAME |

ADDRESS

| | |
|---|---|
| APT.# | CITY |

| | |
|---|---|
| STATE/PROV. | ZIP/POSTAL CODE |

| 7 | 7 | 7 | **Worth TWO FREE BOOKS plus a BONUS Mystery Gift!** |
| 🍒 | 🍒 | 🍒 | **Worth TWO FREE BOOKS!** |
| ♣ | ♣ | ♣ | **Worth ONE FREE BOOK!** |
| 🔔 | 🔔 | 🍒 | **TRY AGAIN!** |

*Visit us online at www.eHarlequin.com*

(S-SE-01/03)

*DETACH AND MAIL CARD TODAY!*

If offer card is missing write to: Silhouette Reader Service, 3010 Walden Ave., P.O. Box 1867, Buffalo NY 14240-1867

# BUSINESS REPLY MAIL
FIRST-CLASS MAIL    PERMIT NO. 717-003    BUFFALO, NY

POSTAGE WILL BE PAID BY ADDRESSEE

SILHOUETTE READER SERVICE
3010 WALDEN AVE
PO BOX 1867
BUFFALO NY 14240-9952

NO POSTAGE
NECESSARY
IF MAILED
IN THE
UNITED STATES

Funny, that wasn't his most pressing question.

He knew that she had to be around thirty, maybe a couple of years older. She was smart, successful, pretty and sexy as hell. But right now she looked ready to jump out of her skin with nerves and embarrassment. Because of him? He would like to think he got to her that much, but he had a feeling that might be wishful thinking on his part.

"You're attractive," he said, wondering if she really didn't know why he'd wanted to kiss her. "Very attractive and I enjoy your company. I had a pretty universal male reaction to both of those facts."

She pressed her lips together and nodded. "Okay," she said, her voice almost a squeak. She cleared her throat again. "So you're talking about, um, you know, interest."

Sex. He was talking about sex. "Interest works, but only if it's returned."

This time there was no question that she was blushing. Her cheeks flushed to a bright red and she nearly dropped her coffee cup.

"I'm not really used to talking to adults," she said in a low voice. "Men, I mean. I don't think I was very good at it before and the lack of practice has only made me worse."

"Then we'll take it slow. The conversation, I mean."

Her eyes widened slightly. "Okay. Well, then I should probably start at the beginning."

He had no idea what she meant. "The beginning?"

"Yeah. I met Marty my last year of college. I was so thrilled to be out on my own and not responsible for anyone but myself. I'd dated some, but hadn't fallen for anyone before. Not like I did with Marty. Everything was so exciting. Marty…'' She sighed. ''He was a few years older. Charming, funny. He'd switched majors so many times that he was still a junior after five years of school. I remember thinking that he was so full of life and so interested in me.''

She looked at him. ''I told you my parents are artists, but what I didn't tell you was that their art is the most important thing in their lives. I remember growing up knowing that no skinned knee, no problem with a friend could ever compete with the perfect light on the right view. While they painted, I didn't exist.''

''Marty was different?''

''I thought so. He focused so intently on me that I didn't realize I was just the latest in a long line of fleeting passions. He swept me off my feet and I married him less than two months later. Within six weeks, I realized I'd married someone just like my parents.''

Nash leaned toward her. ''In what way?''

''He wasn't responsible. He wasn't willing to think about anyone but himself. He didn't care if the bills got paid on time or if they turned off our electricity. He didn't worry about showing up to work on time. There were so many other fun things to be doing. I'm sure a mental health professional wouldn't be surprised that I'd replaced my parents with someone exactly like them, but it was a shock to me. I was devastated.''

He wanted to reach across the table and take her

hands in his, but he didn't. Instead he sipped his coffee, then asked, "Why didn't you leave?"

"I wanted to," she admitted. "I considered my options, thought about what I wanted and decided that I wasn't going through that again. But right before I packed up to go, I found out I was pregnant with Brett."

She moved her cup around on the table. "Marty was thrilled. He swore everything was going to be different, and I wanted to believe him. I thought it would be wrong to take his child away from him, so I stayed. He went from job to job, city to city, state to state, and we went with him. Every time I managed to save a few dollars, he spent them on something crazy like an old beat-up motorcycle or a weekend of river rafting. I waited for him to grow up, to realize he had responsibilities. I found creative ways to make money at home. After a few years, I told him we couldn't continue that way. I would homeschool Brett through kindergarten, but if we weren't settled by the time he was in first grade, I was leaving."

She leaned back in her chair and shrugged. "Brett was three. That gave Marty another three years to get his act together. In the meantime, I started taking night courses whenever I could. Business, mostly. If I had to leave, I wanted to be prepared. Once Brett was of school age, I knew I would be able to take care of us both."

"Then the twins came along," he said.

"Another unplanned pregnancy," she agreed. "Suddenly I had a four-year-old and infant twins. There wasn't any money. I had to pay the doctor off in weekly installments. The week I brought the twins home, the city turned off our electricity. It was hell. Through it all Marty said we'd be just fine. He kept not showing up for work or quitting. About a year later, I snapped. I packed up the kids and I left him. I knew that it would be hard on my own, but caring for three children was a whole lot easier than caring for four.''

If Marty hadn't been dead, Nash would have found him and beaten his sorry butt into the ground.

''He followed me and begged me to come back.'' She looked at Nash, then away. ''Brett adored him. I gave in. I didn't love him anymore, but I felt guilty for leaving. Isn't that crazy? So I stayed. Then one day he got a letter from a lawyer. One that said he'd inherited a bunch of money. I told Marty I wanted to put it on a house. I thought if we could have that much security, I could stand the rest. We were passing through Glenwood at the time, so we decided to buy here. But Marty couldn't just buy a regular house and own it outright. This monstrosity fit right into his dreamworld. I thought it was better than just blowing the money on a sailboat so we could go around the world and I agreed. Then he died.''

Nash didn't know what to say. ''You've done a hell of a job.''

''I've done my best to think about my boys. I want them to be happy and secure. I want them to know they're important to me. None of which is my point.''

She squared her shoulders. ''I'm thirty-three. I've been responsible for someone else since I was old enough to order groceries on the telephone. By the time I was ten, I was paying all the bills and managing the household money. My parents took off for

France when I was twelve. They were gone for five months. I was scared to be by myself for that long, but I got through it. I was the grown-up with Marty and I'm the grown-up now. My point is, I'm not looking for another responsibility. I've heard that men can be partners in some relationships, but I've never seen it.''

Nash heard the words, but he wasn't sure why she was telling him. He added her parents to the list of people he would like to have words with, but that didn't help.

''I'm impressed by how well you've held it all together,'' he said.

She nodded. ''But you don't know why I'm telling you all this.''

''Right.''

She sucked in a breath and stared at the table. ''That kiss last night was pretty incredible. The fact that you didn't go running screaming from the room when you saw me this morning tells me that you maybe didn't mind it too much.''

He knew this was difficult for her, but he couldn't help laughing. ''You're understating my position,'' he said. ''I wanted you. I still want you.''

Her mouth formed an ''oh'' but no sound emerged. She glanced at him, her eyes wide and stunned.

''That's clear,'' she whispered. ''I, ah, appreciate your honesty. The thing is, I haven't allowed myself to have a sexual thought since Marty's death. I don't meet many men, but the ones I do meet either take off at the thought of a woman with three kids, or they're too much like Marty and I'm the one run-

ning. I don't want a relationship. I don't want to get
involved. But..."

Her voice trailed off.

Nash leaned toward her. He wasn't sure what direction she was heading, but if it was the one he
thought...where could he sign up?

"I thought that part of me was dead," she said.
"It's not."

"Good to know."

She smiled slightly. "I thought so. And that made
me wonder, what with you leaving town at the end
of next week and all..."

He put the pieces together, rearranged them and
did it again. He came up with the same answer.
Which meant he was doing it wrong. No way his
luck was that good.

She stared at him. "You really need to talk now."

"You want me to say it?"

She nodded.

If he got it wrong, she would throw her coffee in
his face and he'd be forced to look for new quarters.
He could live with that. If this was going to be his
fantasy, too, he might as well just go for it and prepare himself to be shot down.

"You're not interested in a relationship," he said.

"Right."

"You liked the kiss."

"Uh-huh."

"A lot."

She grinned. "A lot works."

"What you're looking for is something more
along those lines. An affair while I'm in town and
when I leave, it's over. No strings, no regrets, no
broken hearts. Until then, we keep each other company at night. Am I close?"

## Chapter Eight

He was close, Stephanie thought as embarrassment and horror swirled in her throat. So close that he'd grasped the concept in one seemingly easy try.

It was one thing to *think* about hot monkey sex with a virtual stranger who happened to be handsome, hunky and heart-poundingly erotic, it was another to have the object of her desire figure it all out and say it back to her. Out loud.

In the light of day, the idea sounded sleazy and off-putting and completely improbable.

Without thinking, she pushed herself to her feet and bolted from the room. She had no particular destination in mind—just a need to be away from Nash.

As she raced along the hall, she tried to tell herself that she hadn't done anything wrong. She was an adult, Nash was an adult. He'd kissed her and they'd both liked it. So what was the big deal about suggesting taking things to the next level? Didn't people do that all the time?

Maybe, she thought frantically. But not her. She'd been with exactly one man in her life—her husband. The rules and social mores of the modern dating world were completely beyond her. She had never asked a man to hold her hand before, much less ask him to have an affair.

She reached the bottom stair, but before she could put her foot on it, someone grabbed her arm.

She stopped and sucked in a breath. Okay—not someone. Nash. She ducked her head because she could feel heat on her cheeks. Not only from what he'd figured out about what she wanted, but because running hadn't exactly been mature.

Silence stretched between them, lengthening like taffy. Finally it snapped with an almost-audible crack and he spoke.

"I apologize," he said quietly. "Apparently I misread the situation and insulted you."

His words were so at odds with what she'd been thinking, she couldn't help turning around and staring at him. His dark gaze settled on her face as he shrugged.

"Wishful thinking on my part," he said. "I projected what I wanted onto you."

He was taking the fall for this? She couldn't believe it. "I... You..." She blinked. "Projecting?"

"The kiss was hot. It made me want more."

She processed the statement. The ripples of horror changed to tingles of excitement as she considered the possibilities. "You don't mind that I'm inter-

ested in a no-strings affair? You don't think that's
tacky and cheap and sleazy of me?''

His mouth curved into a slow smile as fire flared
in his irises. "Do I look like I mind?" He released
her arm and reached up to stroke her cheek. "You're
attractive, sexy and you kiss like a wet-dream fantasy come to life."

Oh, my. Speaking of wet, his words made her go
all squishy inside. An ache began between her thighs
and spread out in every direction. She felt both weak
and incredibly powerful. Desire swept through her—
the kind of desire she'd hadn't felt in what seemed
like a lifetime.

"Why don't you ask your question again," she
said. "I'll try not to run this time."

His expression tightened and grew more intense.
Around them, the air thickened as tension crackled.
She could feel the hairs on her arms and the back
of her neck standing up. Her gaze locked with his.

"Are you interested in an affair?" he asked, his
voice low and heavy with what she was pretty sure
was sexual need. "Sex, fun and when my time in
town is up, we both walk away. No regrets. No ex-
pectations."

It sounded wicked. It sounded perfect.

"Yes," she whispered. "That's exactly what I
want."

She couldn't believe she'd spoken the words
aloud, but before she could give in to self-doubt, he
pulled her close.

"It's what I want, too," he murmured. "I've been
hearing rumors for years, and I finally get to find
out if they're true."

Rumors? "About me?"

He pressed his mouth against her neck. Delicious tingles tiptoed down her spine, making it nearly impossible to think.

"Not you specifically," he told her. "Older women."

Stephanie had already placed her hands on his shoulders and if his thick muscles didn't feel so good as she pressed her fingers against him, she would have snatched them back. Instead she shifted a little, without actually breaking contact with his hard body.

"Older women?"

He raised his head and grinned. "You said you're thirty-three. I'm thirty-one. Ever since I first figured out the possibilities between a man and a woman, I've been hearing stories about how great it is to be with an older woman. All that experience. All that latent desire as they reach their sexual peak. I've always wondered if everything they say is true."

She supposed there were two ways to respond to his challenge. Duck and run, or challenge him back. While her first inclination was to do the former, something told her there was more fun to be had in the latter.

"Of course it's true," she said as she leaned close. "I hope you can keep up."

He gave a low, throaty laugh right before he claimed her mouth.

The hot, hungry kiss took her breath away. His lips pressed against hers with enough pressure to make her a hundred percent sure he wanted her as much as she wanted him. She parted instantly and he swept inside.

He tasted of coffee and sin. She shivered in

delight at the first brush of intimate contact. Heat poured through her, making her legs weak and her breathing catch. Need exploded, surrounding her, crashing over her, making her want with a desperation that left her ravenous and achingly alive.

As she tilted her head to deepen the kiss, he pulled her closer still. They touched everywhere. Her breasts flattened against his chest, his arousal throbbed along her belly. His hands roamed her back, moving up and down in a rhythm that matched the pounding of her heart.

While she traced the breadth of his shoulders, he explored her waist, then her hips. One hand slipped to her rear and squeezed. His fingertips just grazed the very top of the back of her thigh. The light contact shouldn't have been anything special, yet it burned through her clothes and singed her skin.

Unexpectedly Nash bit down on her lower lip. She gasped. When he drew the sensitized skin into his mouth and gently sucked, the gasp turned into a moan.

They had to get closer, she thought, need turning frantic. Closer and naked and touching. Now. This instant.

The message traveled from her brain to her hands. Even as he shifted so that his fingers grazed her nipples and jolts of wanting arrowed down to the thick swollen dampness between her legs, she tugged at his shirt. The fabric pulled free of his waistband. She fumbled with buttons, unfastening the first two. He slipped his hands under her sweater. She caught her breath in anticipation. His large, warm hands cupped her breasts.

Her thin bra felt like a steel barrier keeping him

from touching bare skin. Torn between wanting to get his shirt off him and wanting to feel his skin on hers, she tried to shimmy out of her sweater while still unbuttoning his shirt. At the same time, she turned and bumped the bottom stair with her foot.

Nash caught her as she started to fall. His strong arms held her upright.

"We need to take this upstairs," he murmured as he kissed along her jaw to her left ear.

"Okay."

Her head fell back in supplication. She silently begged him never to stop. His hands returned to her breasts and she couldn't think…couldn't do anything but feel. It was all too good, too amazing, too incredible. The wet heat of his mouth, the way he flicked his tongue against the sensitive skin below her ear. Then there were his fingers and the way they teased and played and pressed against her nipples. Not hard, not soft. Just right. Very right.

"Stephanie?"

"Uh-huh?"

"Hang on."

He swept her up in his arms, just like Rhett Butler carrying Scarlett. After an initial moment of being disconcerted, she felt light and feminine and too sexy for words.

"I wish I was naked right now," she said.

His dark eyes brightened with need. "Me, too. My room's closer. Is that all right?"

She couldn't answer because he was kissing her, but she tried to tell him "yes" with her lips and her tongue. Apparently he got the message because the next thing she knew, they were on the second floor and heading down the hall.

He pushed open his door and stepped inside. The blinds were open and sunlight filtered through the lacy curtains. The door bumped closed behind them, then they were next to the bed and she was sliding to her feet.

The second she felt firm footing beneath her, she wrapped her arms around his neck and leaned against him. He hauled her close and deepened the kiss.

Every part of her body screamed for his touch, for nakedness, for release. She tried to kick off her shoes, but her brain wouldn't focus on anything but the feel of his mouth against hers and refused to send messages to muscles. Nash fumbled with his shirt, then chuckled.

"We're not making progress," he said as he broke the kiss and took a half step back.

He finished unfastening buttons and shrugged out of his shirt. She managed to slip off her shoes and reach for the hem of her sweater. But before she could pull it off, he bent low and kissed the bare skin below her bra band. Soft, damp kisses tickled along her ribs. Savoring the delicate caress, she froze with her hands clutching her sweater, her arms half-above her head. He cupped her breasts, then reached for her sweater and finished the job.

He returned his mouth to hers and kissed her. As he teased her tongue, he unfastened her bra and pulled the straps down her arms.

Her already taut nipples brushed against the hair on his chest. The contact both tickled and aroused. Every part of her was so hyper-sensitized that she desperately wanted more of everything. She clung to his shoulders and turned her torso back and forth so her nipples slid against his bare skin. At the same time she sucked hard on his tongue and pressed her belly to his arousal.

Nash groaned low in his throat, brought his hands up to cup her breasts and rubbed her nipples with his thumbs. Pleasure spiraled through her chest, then dove deep and landed between her thighs. Heat increased, as did the swelling. She was so ready, she thought desperately. They were both still half-dressed and she was shaking with need.

She dropped her hands to her waistband and unfastened her slacks. He followed her actions, which moved them closer to naked, but left her breasts wanting more.

In a matter of seconds, she'd pulled off the rest of her clothes. Nash pushed down his jeans and briefs, tugged off his socks, then gave her a brief kiss, followed by the command "Don't move."

He disappeared into the bathroom. She heard fumbling, three swear words, then something hard fell on the floor. He reappeared holding a box of condoms.

The sight of birth control should have been sobering, but Stephanie was too far gone for rational thought. She didn't want to know how or why he'd been prepared, but she was grateful.

When he rejoined her, he tossed the condoms onto the nightstand, then urged her to sit on the bed. From there he eased her onto her back and knelt next to her. One leg slipped between hers. As he bent low and took her right nipple in his mouth, he pushed his rock-hard thigh up against her waiting dampness.

The combination of the pulling, sucking kiss and the pressure against her pulsing need nearly sent her over the edge. She gasped wordlessly and dug her fingers into his hair.

''Don't stop,'' she breathed, not wanting either point of contact to end. She pulsed her hips shamelessly, rubbing herself against him, squirming to get closer, to get the pressure higher, faster, harder.

He switched his attention to her other breast and shifted so he knelt between her legs. He moved his leg, then replaced it with his hand.

Strong, sure fingers slipped between her curls into slick flesh. He explored all of her, brushing against that single point of pleasure in a way that made her suck in her breath in anticipation. Then he shifted slightly and slid two fingers inside her.

She felt words leave her lips, but couldn't say what they were. She couldn't do anything but feel the way he moved in and out of her. Hot need pooled, then grew, then spilled over into every cell of her body. She barely noticed when he stopped kissing her breasts and instead pressed his mouth against her belly. He moved lower and lower, shifting back with each kiss, yet continuing to move his fingers inside her.

With his free hand, he parted her curls, then placed his mouth directly over that one most-sensitive spot and gently licked her.

Air spilled from her lungs. Before she could catch her breath, he closed his lips around her and gently sucked. At the same time he flicked his tongue back and forth, and moved his fingers and then she was flying.

Her orgasm was as powerful as it was unexpected. She shook and gasped and moaned and dug her heels into the mattress. Spasms rippled through her as pleasure eased the tension that had been plaguing her for what felt like a century. He continued to touch her, softening his kiss, moving his fingers more slowly, but still filling her, taking her on and on until it seemed that she'd been climaxing for hours.

At last her body relaxed and he stilled. Stephanie felt as if her bones had melted. She might never be able to walk again, but did it matter? Did anything matter but the delightful lethargy stealing over her?

Nash pressed a kiss to her inner thigh, then shifted so he was lying next to her. He was smiling.

"I don't have to ask if that worked for you," he teased.

"Probably not. If there's a story on the news about an earthquake in the area, I guess I'm going to have to take responsibility. Or maybe it's your fault."

"I like it being my fault."

She touched his face, then brushed her thumb across his mouth. "That was amazing."

"I'm glad."

She turned toward him and put her hand on his hip, then slid it down to his large erection. "Ready for act two?"

Instead of answering, he reached for the box of condoms. While he opened the package, she leaned over him and kissed him. At the first brush of his tongue on hers, tension returned to her body. She deepened the kiss, then pulled back to lightly bite her way along his jaw.

"You're distracting me," he grumbled.

"Really?" She glanced down to watch as he fumbled with the protection. "Want help?"

"Sure. I was never good with these."

She took the condom from him and gently slid it down his arousal. "Does the unopened package mean you haven't been practicing much?" she asked.

His dark gaze settled on her face. "I haven't been with anyone since my wife passed away. I met someone a few months ago and thought maybe..." His voice trailed off. "I bought the condoms because of that, but things ended long before we got to the naked stage."

She supposed that her friends would tell her it was dangerous to be a man's first time after the death of his wife. Of course, Nash was her first time, too. Besides, they'd agreed on a no-commitment sexual attachment. She liked him, she wanted him, and glory be if he didn't feel exactly the same. It was the perfect relationship.

"Ready to take that latex for a test-drive?" she asked.

"Sure."

She started to slip onto her back, but he put his hands on her hips and urged her to get on top. After swinging her leg over his hips, she settled above him. He brought both his hands up to her breasts and cupped her curves. The second his thumbs brushed against her nipples, she felt her insides clench. Apparently he wasn't the only one ready for round two.

She reached between her legs and grasped his hardness, then pressed the tip of him against her wetness. As she pulled her hand away, she eased down onto him.

Her body had to stretch slightly to accommodate

his thickness. Nerve endings quivered as he filled every bit of her. She braced herself and began to move.

The feeling was too good, she thought as her muscles clenched hard around him. Each time she slid down over him, she felt herself tensing more and more. His hands on her breasts only pushed her closer to the edge.

"You're holding back," he said, his voice sounding strained.

She opened her eyes and saw the tension on his face. He was watching her.

"Just give in," he told her.

"I want to." She sucked in a breath as a ripple of pleasure cascaded through her. "It's just..."

"You think I'm going to complain if you come again?"

She smiled. "Good point."

He stared at her. "Come on. I want to feel you. Just let go."

With each thrust of him filling her, she found herself getting closer and closer. Soon there wasn't going to be anything to talk about.

"Do it."

He accompanied his command with a rapid pulse of his hips. The hands on her breasts moved more quickly. He filled her again and again until the need grew to an unbearable pitch. She sat up and put her hands on her thighs, then raised and lowered herself faster and faster.

Nash figured this was one of life's most perfect moments. He was seconds from his own release, but he was damn sure going to hold back until Stephanie climaxed. Unfortunately his good intentions were severely tested by the sight of her riding him up and down like some X-rated cowgirl. With each shift of her body, her breasts bounced up and down, drawing his gaze and making his mouth water with desire. She had her head back, her eyes closed and she was lost in the pleasure of the moment. It was about the most erotic situation he'd ever experienced.

He could feel pressure building deep and low, which only meant trouble. He tried to think of something else, but how could he with her naked and bouncing, with her mouth parting slightly and her tongue sweeping across her lower lip as she—

He groaned as his release exploded from him. White-hot pleasure swept through him in a fury of rushing pleasure. He remained conscious enough to notice that she'd cried out at the exact moment he'd lost it. Even through the waves of his orgasm, he felt her body contracting around him, pulling every drop from him, making him come longer than he'd thought possible.

When they'd recovered enough for her to crawl off him and him to clean up, they slipped under the covers and lay on their sides looking at each other.

Stephanie smiled at him. Nash liked how contentment showed itself in the lines of her face and the way her knee nestled casually between his. He liked the scent of her body mingling with the fragrance of their lovemaking, and he liked how, even though they'd just finished, he wanted to make love with her again.

It had been a long time, he thought. Too long. After Tina had died, he hadn't set out to avoid women and sex. Somehow it had just happened.

He'd buried himself in work and had never found his way out.

"What are you thinking?" she asked.

"That I never meant to live as a monk after my wife died."

"I'm surprised the single women in the office didn't make a play for you."

"How do you know they didn't?"

Her smile widened. "Do you have to beat them off with a stick?"

"Only a couple of times a year."

She looked away and the smile faded. "You must still love her very much."

The transition confused him for about a minute, then he figured out what she wanted to know.

"Hey." He touched her chin, forcing her gaze back to his face. "You and I were the only ones in this bed. At least on my side."

The smile returned. "On my side, too. I haven't been with anyone since Marty, but that's not about being brokenhearted. As I was trying to explain before, things were complicated."

He slid his hand under the sheet and cupped the curve of her bare hip. Her skin was like warm silk.

"Is this easy?" he asked.

"Very. The best kind of easy."

He agreed. In the past, he'd found the first sexual encounter in any relationship about as dangerous as a minefield. There were too many ways to misstep. But with Stephanie, everything had fallen into place. He'd never had a sex-only, no-strings affair before, but so far it was better than he could have hoped.

"How about a few ground rules to keep things that way," he said.

She nodded and sat up. "Good idea."

As she'd moved, the sheet had fallen away from her breasts. He found his attention sliding from her words to her body. He leaned toward her and touched his finger to the outer curve of her breast, then traced a line to the place where that pale skin darkened to a deep rose. Her nipple instantly tightened. After licking the tip of his finger, he brushed his damp skin against her nipple and waited for her breath to catch.

Damn if it didn't. As expected, his body responded with a rush of blood heading south.

"Rule number one," she said. "Lots of sex."

He raised his head slightly to look at her face. "That's a good rule. So good we should probably make it one and two."

"Fair enough. Sex and lots of it. You're only in town for a short period of time. I want to take advantage of that."

"My kind of woman."

He wanted nothing more than to lean in close enough to kiss her breasts, but figured they had better get things settled before the next round. He forced himself to drop his hand to his side and focus on the conversation.

"I'm going to assume you don't want the boys to know about us," he said.

She nodded slowly. "It would only confuse them. Brett still worries about me replacing his father and the twins would only want to bond with you."

"So I'll leave my door unlocked. You can head downstairs when you're ready to have your way with me."

"That works. We'll also have during the day until

school's out at the end of the week. If you're not too busy with your family.''

''I'm not.'' He reached for her hand and laced their fingers together. ''Speaking of my family, would you mind joining me for a few of the bigger get-togethers? You and the boys?''

He wasn't sure why he made the request and he hoped she wouldn't ask him to explain.

Luck was on his side. She nodded right away. ''That would be great. I had a good time and I know my kids did, too. All that family can be a little intimidating.''

''I'm not intimidated.''

''Because you're a big tough guy.''

''You know it.''

She laughed, then slipped down on the mattress. ''Okay, then I'll think of it as helping out. Sort of 'you scratch my itch and I'll scratch yours.'''

''I like the sound of that.'' He moved closer and drew back the sheet, baring her to the waist. ''So where does it itch?''

She wrapped her arms around his neck and kissed him. ''Everywhere.''

## Chapter Nine

Stephanie had never considered painting a room anything but a chore, yet this afternoon she found herself humming while she worked. Suddenly the squishy swish of the roller on the walls sounded cheerful and lively. The smell didn't bother her, not with the gatehouse windows wide open and the afternoon sun spilling into the room. Even the low-grade complaining of long-unused muscles didn't do anything to dampen her happy mood. She doubted anything short of a serious disaster could wipe the smile off her face.

Life was good, she thought as she smoothed the pale paint over the prepared wall. Life was damn good.

She giggled softly and stretched up her arm. The movement pulled at her hips, which ached from being extended when she'd parted her legs as wide as possible so she could wrap them around Nash. The discomfort only added to her exuberance. Being sore after something boring like an exercise class wasn't very inspiring, but being sore because of mind-clearing sex with an incredible lover was worth every twinge. Her insides still tingled with lingering aftershocks and she couldn't stop sighing with contentment. While she'd never considered herself an affair kind of girl, obviously this was something she should have done years ago.

"It never crossed my mind," she murmured aloud.

With three kids and a pretty hefty mortgage, she'd been more concerned about staying afloat financially after Marty's death than getting any sexual needs met. After a while it had been easy to forget she even had needs. Making love with her husband had been very nice, but over time, the memory faded. She didn't want another relationship with a man, so she'd figured intimacy was no longer available to her.

Until Nash had shown her all the possibilities. And what possibilities there were. They'd made love twice, then agreed to try and get some work done. It had been all of three hours since they'd left his bed and she couldn't wait to get back into it.

Mentally calculating the time until the boys would be turning in for the night, she wondered how she would survive that long without Nash touching her. Now that she knew he was even better than her fantasies, she wanted to take advantage of every second they had together.

"You're not working," Nash said as he walked

in from the kitchen. "You're standing on the ladder, grinning."

She laughed. "If I tell you that I'm thinking about us being together will that make it okay?"

"Absolutely."

He leaned against the door frame, a tall, good-looking man holding spackle and a putty knife. He'd pulled on a dark blue T-shirt over worn jeans. She liked how he was competent in whatever he did, whether it was patching a wall or making her scream with pleasure. She liked how he was comfortable asking her what she liked when they were in bed, and offering to help out around the house when they weren't. She liked that he was a bit nervous about being around his new family and that he wanted her there to act as a buffer. Not that he'd ever said the latter, but she'd read between the lines.

What she liked most was that they were equals. He had needs, she had needs. No one was more in charge. No one was subservient. They were taking care of each other, while getting what they wanted.

She dipped the roller into the paint on the tray. "How's the patching coming?" she asked.

"All done in the kitchen." He turned his attention to the walls. "Are you sure you don't want me to do the painting in here? You're kind of short to reach the top of the walls."

"That's why they invented ladders," she said. "I like doing this. If you want to help, you're welcome to paint the windows. I already taped the glass, but I haven't started on the frames yet."

"Sure. Let me put this away."

He covered the can of spackle, then set it on the makeshift workbench she'd created by placing a flat door over two wooden crates. After he left, she heard running water. The man cleaned up after himself, she thought happily. Did it get any better than that?

Nash returned and took a nearly empty gallon can of paint and a brush, then walked over to the large window. She watched him expertly brush the wood trim.

"So how did an FBI negotiator learn how to paint?" she asked.

"I helped paint our house a few times when I was growing up. Since then I've been dragged into a couple of projects with guys from work."

"Do you like your job?"

He glanced at her then returned his attention to the window. "Most of the time. Not when it goes bad."

She didn't know all that much about what he did, but knew it had a lot to do with negotiating with criminals holding hostages. A bad day for him would mean someone died.

"How did you get in that line of work?"

He shrugged. "I was recruited by the FBI out of college. I worked in Dallas for a while, got my master's in psychology. I went into profiling, then I attended a lecture by a negotiator. I trained, worked with him for a while and figured out it was something I had the temperament for."

"Meaning you can handle high-stress situations?"

"That and disconnect from the emotions inherent in the incident."

Low-key and distant, she thought. He'd been that way with his family at the pizza-night dinner.

Friendly, but not completely involved. She envied him his emotional detachment. If she'd been able to muster a little for herself, she might have been able to leave Marty.

"So you were probably really annoying when your wife wanted to pick a fight," she said. "There she'd be, all crabby and on edge, and you'd be rational and logical."

She'd been teasing, but instead of smiling at her words Nash looked thoughtful.

"We were different," he admitted as he continued to paint the window frame. "Tina lived on the emotional edge most of the time. Drama fueled her. I never figured she would make it as an agent."

Stephanie nearly dropped her roller. She grabbed the handle with both hands and tried not to look shocked. "She was an FBI agent?"

Nash nodded.

Who would have known? Stephanie hadn't much thought about his late wife, but if she had, she would have assumed the woman was a… She frowned, not sure what she would have assumed. Certainly not a federal agent.

"We met during training. I was one of her instructors. I thought she was too impulsive and wanted to flunk her out. I was outvoted."

She turned back to the wall and resumed painting. Better to leave a few streaks on the walls than to stand on the ladder with her mouth open. "Not a very romantic beginning," she said.

"It wasn't. I thought she was a flake, and she thought I was a hard-nosed rule follower. She moved on and I forgot about her. We hooked up about a year later, on assignment."

Doing something dangerous, she thought wistfully. Capturing bad guys or saving innocent lives. There was tension, adrenaline followed by passion.

Stephanie didn't like the knot that formed in her stomach or the feeling of being a fairly typical, fairly boring thirty-something single mom.

"If you two were married, you must have changed your initial opinions of each other," she said.

Nash shrugged. "We were always opposites."

"Sometimes that works."

"It didn't for you and Marty."

That was true. "I'm not sure we were opposites so much as we wanted different things," she said, thinking it was safer to think about her late husband than Nash's late wife. "Or maybe it was just that I wasn't willing to pay the price for always doing what I wanted. I didn't like always having to be the grown-up, but Marty didn't seem to give me a choice. Someone had to make sure the bills got paid on time and that there was food in the house. But there were times when I envied his ability not to worry about things like money and consequences. I could never let go that much."

"You took on a lot at an early age. I think kids who have to grow up fast never forget what it was like to be young and in charge. I had the same thing at home. My mom worked a lot of hours and my brother was a complete screwup. He was born to break rules. Even though we were twins, I always felt like the oldest."

"But he grew out of it," she said. "Kevin's a U.S. Marshal now." Kevin had changed. Grown up. Most people did. Just not Marty.

Nash turned around and looked at her. "How did this conversation get so serious? People having an affair aren't supposed to talk about anything significant."

She smiled. "I didn't know. This is my first affair, so you'll have to fill me in on all the rules."

He set the brush on the edge of the paint can and walked toward her. "The rules are whatever we want them to be."

"Really?"

There was a light in his dark eyes that made her insides quiver. As he approached, she put the roller onto the tray and leaned down. The kiss was hard, hot and left her breathless. Wanting exploded within her. She wrapped her arms around his neck and let him lower her to the ground.

"It's been less than three hours and I want you again," he murmured against her mouth. "At this rate we're not going to get a lot of work done."

"I don't mind."

"Good, because I—"

A noise caught their attention. Both she and Nash turned. Stephanie cringed when she saw Brett standing in the open doorway of the gatehouse. The look on his face told her that he'd seen her in Nash's arms and that he felt betrayed. Before she could say anything, he took off for the house.

Desire drained out of her, leaving behind guilt and confusion. On the one hand, she was glad that Brett remembered his father and still thought about him. On the other hand, while she wasn't looking for love or anything close to it, she knew it wasn't right for her to close off that part of her life simply because her twelve-year-old son might not approve. Brett had to learn that it was okay to move on with life. But was this the time to have that conversation? And if so, what was she going to say? Complicating the situation was the fact that she and Nash didn't have a relationship she could explain to her children.

There was no one to ask, she thought sadly. No one to share her worries with. Like most tough times in her life, she was going to have to wing it and hope she didn't mess up too badly.

She took a step toward the house, then stopped when Nash touched her arm.

"Brett's upset," he said.

"I know."

"Maybe this would be better discussed with a guy."

Stephanie stared at him. "You want to talk to Brett about what he saw?"

"*Want* is a little strong, but I have an idea about what he's feeling. I'm not going to tell him what's going on between us, but I can reassure him."

She considered the offer. The mature side of her argued that Brett was *her* child and *her* responsibility. While Nash was probably a nice guy and definitely great in bed, he didn't have children of his own and he had only known hers for a few days. Therefore she should be the one to make things right with her son. The rest of her wanted to toss the problem in his lap and let him solve it. Just once it would be nice not to have to sweat the right thing to say.

"I really should talk to him," she said.

Nash lightly kissed her. "Go paint," he told her. "Give me ten minutes. If I'm not back by then, come find us."

Letting go was unfamiliar. Releasing responsibility was unheard of. Stephanie battled what was right with what was easy. Before she'd made a decision, Nash left the gatehouse.

Ten minutes, she told herself as she checked her watch. He couldn't mess up too badly in that amount of time, could he?

Nash walked into the house and paused to listen. When he heard something thump against the floor, he headed for the kitchen rather than the stairs.

When he pushed open the door, he found Brett banging his way through emptying the dishwasher. The kid's shoulders were slumped and stark pain darkened his blue eyes.

"Hey," he said. "How's it going?"

The twelve-year-old spun to glare at him. "You don't belong here," Brett yelled. "You're a guest. Guests stay in the public rooms. Not the kitchen. The kitchen is for family. Get out."

Nash closed the door behind him and approached the boy. Brett clutched a pot in his hands as if he would use it as a weapon if he had to.

"Did you hear me?" the kid demanded.

"I heard all of it. Even what you didn't say."

Nash recognized the boy's helplessness, the frustration that fueled anger. He knew Brett wanted to be big enough and strong enough to force Nash out of the room, the house and his mother's life. Brett wanted Nash never to have come here, never to have existed. Now that he was here, Brett wanted him gone.

The old feelings were still there, Nash thought with some surprise as he took a seat at the table.

Buried, nearly forgotten, but still real. How many times had he wanted to take on Howard? Bad enough when Howard and his mother had just been dating, it had gone worse when the two had announced their engagement and said Howard would be adopting the boys. Like they were babies. Like they needed him.

"Your mom's a real nice lady," Nash said slowly, searching for the right words, trying to remember what would have made him feel better. "Pretty, a lot of fun."

He glanced at Brett and gave a slight smile. "She probably seems old to you, but not to me. I like her a lot."

Fear flashed in Brett's eyes. Nash leaned forward and rested his elbows on his knees.

"The thing is, I'm just passing through," he said. "I'm not sticking around. In a couple of weeks I'll go back to Chicago. That's where I live and work. That's where my life is."

His life? For the first time since Tina's death Nash realized he was lying about having anything close to a life. He had a job and that was about it. Few friends outside of work. None that he socialized with. He lived alone and he was damned tired of it.

He shook off that train of thought. Later, he told himself. Right now Brett was more important.

"I understand what you're going through," Nash said.

Brett turned away. "Yeah, right."

"Okay. Grown-ups say that all the time. It's boring and annoying, huh? But in this case, it's true. Your dad died. My dad never bothered to stick around after he got my mom pregnant. There was just her, Kevin and me. She was really young and didn't have any money, so it was hard for her. She worked a lot. She worried a lot. I hated to see that, so I filled in when I could. Sort of like you with the twins.''

Brett traced a pattern on the countertop. Nash wasn't sure, but he thought the kid might be listening.

''They're still pretty young,'' he continued, ''but *you* understand that it's hard for her. You worry. And the last thing you need is some guy coming in to mess up your family.''

Brett looked at him in surprise.

Nash nodded. ''It happened to us. My mom started dating this guy—Howard. He was okay, I guess. But I never really trusted him. Why was he butting in? He didn't belong.''

''What happened?'' Brett asked.

''They got married. I didn't want them to, but they did anyway.''

There was more to the story, but Nash didn't bother going into it. He'd made his point.

''I'm not like that,'' he told Brett. ''I like your mom and I'd like to see her while I'm in town. But I *am* leaving, so all this is temporary. I'm not looking to get married or to replace your dad. I wanted you to know that, man-to-man.''

He waited while Brett considered the information. Then the kid sucked in a breath.

''Okay. I get it.'' He still looked troubled, but not so afraid. ''I guess my mom needs someone to talk to and stuff.'' He gaze narrowed. ''But you shouldn't kiss her where just anyone can see. My brothers wouldn't understand. They don't remember

Dad much and they might think you're sticking around.''

"Good point. I'll remember it." Nash stood. "Something else, Brett. You may not believe me, but it's true. Even if your mom were to find someone she fell in love with and wanted to marry, that doesn't mean the guy would be taking your dad's place. No one can do that. You might even like the guy, which would be okay, too. But your dad will always be your dad.''

Brett looked doubtful, but didn't disagree. Nash figured he'd done as much as he could. He held out his hand.

"Friends?" he asked.

Brett stared at his hand, then him. Finally he moved close and they shook.

"I guess we can be friends," the boy said.

"I'd like that." He jerked his head toward the front of the house. "I'm going back to the gatehouse now, if that's all right with you.''

Brett nodded. "Tell my mom I'm going to get changed, then I'll come help, too.''

"I know she'll appreciate that.''

Brett headed for the door, then paused. Staring at the ground he said, "Thanks for explaining things, Nash.''

"You're welcome.''

Nash returned to the gatehouse and found Stephanie waiting impatiently by the door.

"You nearly hit your limit," she said, glancing from him to her watch. "I was giving you ten minutes, then I was going to barge in and take over.''

She tried to smile as she spoke, but he could see the worry in her eyes.

"We worked it out," he said, then explained what he and Brett had discussed.

When he was done, she sank onto the floor and pulled her knees up to her chest. "Thanks for clearing things up with him. He and I used to be able to talk about anything, but lately I've noticed things are changing. I guess it's because he's getting older. I'm not looking forward to him being a teenager. That's for sure."

"He'll get through it, as will you," he said, crouching next to her. "He's a good kid."

"Too good. Oh, sure, he can be a pain, but for the most part, he really tries to step in and help. Sometimes it's easy to let him. When that happens I do my best to remember he *is* still a kid and not my personal assistant. He's getting to that age when he needs a man around. Sometimes I think I should get over my fear of getting involved with another irresponsible guy and get married simply to take the heat off Brett. It would sure give him a break."

She continued talking, but Nash no longer heard what she was saying. Instead he was remembering a conversation he'd had with his mother shortly after she'd told him she was marrying Howard. He'd protested the engagement, saying they didn't need Howard around. His mother had tried to explain that Howard was a good man whom she loved very much.

"But there's more to it than that," she'd said. "My marrying Howard means you don't have to be the man in the family anymore. You won't have as much responsibility. I want that for you."

At the time he'd felt as if he were being eased out of his own family. Now, looking back, he wondered if his mother had worried about him the same way Stephanie worried about Brett.

Footsteps on the walkway interrupted his musings. Both he and Stephanie stood.

"Anybody home?" a man called.

"Hey, Nash, did your landlady kick you out already?"

He didn't recognize the first voice, but he knew the second.

"Kevin," he said and headed toward the front porch. Nash assumed the other man was one of the Haynes brothers.

When he stepped outside he saw he'd been right. Kevin and Travis stood by the sidewalk. They waved at him and walked closer.

Kevin smiled at Stephanie. "I knew you'd get tired of his ugly face. Threw him out, huh?"

She laughed. "Actually he's helping me patch and paint my gatehouse. He does quality work and if he's at it much longer, I'm going to have to give him a discount on his room."

Kevin shook his head. "Nash getting his hands dirty? I can't believe it."

Nash stepped next to his brother and threw a mock punch. Kevin ducked, shot out a jab, then slapped him on the back. "Wait until you hear what Travis has to say."

Travis Haynes wore a khaki-colored uniform and a beige Stetson. He pulled off the hat and smoothed back his hair.

"Kevin and I were talking," he said. "I happened to mention that once a year the Glenwood sheriff's

department along with local firefighters and para-
medics get together with the army base about fifty
miles from here. We break up into teams and spend
a couple of days playing war games. The more experienced men are paired up with new recruits, giving them a chance to learn. What with your background and all, I thought you might be interested.''

Nash could see Stephanie out of the corner of his
eyes. She stood on Travis's right. At the mention of
war games, she rolled her eyes.

''Gage already said yes,'' Kevin said. ''I did, too.
If Quinn shows up in time, I know he'll be in.''

''I'm in,'' Nash said.

Kevin nudged Travis. ''Told you he'd say yes.''

Nash turned to Stephanie. ''What about you?''

She shook her head. ''I have an actual life that
requires me not to play games. Why is it men refuse
to stop acting like little boys?'' She looked stern,
but her tone was teasing.

''Everybody has to play sometime,'' Nash said.

Her gaze locked with his. He felt the sexual tension return and wished they were alone.

''I like a different kind of game,'' she informed
him, then turned her attention to Kevin and Travis.
''Gentlemen, I need to get back to my painting. I
hope your war games are everything you want them
to be.''

Travis grinned. ''You sound just like my wife.
She makes fun of me every year.''

Stephanie waved and headed back into the gatehouse. Nash watched her go, his gaze drifting from
her trim waist to the sway of her hips. Heat flared
inside him. He knew he had it bad and he didn't

give a damn. Wanting Stephanie was the most fun he'd had in years.

"The war games start in a couple of weeks," Kevin said. "You're going to have to extend your vacation."

Nash thought of all the time off he'd accumulated in the past couple of years. "Not a problem."

"Good."

"We need to—" Travis's cell phone rang, cutting him off. "Just a sec," he said as he pulled out the phone and pushed the Talk button. "Haynes." He walked a couple of steps away as he listened.

Kevin stepped closer and lowered his voice. "So what's with you and Stephanie?"

Nash wasn't surprised his brother had noticed his interest. He and Kevin might not be identical twins, but they were still closer than most brothers and didn't have a lot of trouble knowing what the other was thinking.

Nash looked at the gatehouse. "Nothing significant."

"That's not how it looked from here."

"She's great, but I'm not into permanent relationships. As it turns out, neither is she."

"You can't be alone forever," Kevin said.

"Why not?"

"It's better to be with the right person."

Nash shook his head. "You say that now that you've found Haley, but six months ago you thought alone was a fine way to be."

"You loved Tina enough to want to marry her. What happened that was so bad you wouldn't want to risk trying again?"

"Nothing was bad." Nothing specific. He

couldn't point to any one event and say "this is the reason I don't want to get involved." Probably because his problem wasn't about his marriage. It was about him.

"You're stubborn," Kevin said.

"We have that in common."

"I know. Mom used to complain about it all the time." He took a deep breath. "Speaking of which, I want to invite her and Howard out here for a few days. To meet everyone. I know you're not going to like it, but you're going to have to deal with it. You can't—"

Nash cut him off with a simple, "Fine with me."

Kevin stared at him. "You're serious?"

"Sure. Give them the name of Stephanie's B&B. They can stay here."

Nash thought of his recent revelations about the past. Maybe things hadn't been exactly as he'd remembered them. Maybe being twelve had colored his view of the truth. Maybe it was time to change things.

"Great. I'll call tonight." Kevin grinned. "They're going to like Stephanie."

"Don't go there," Nash growled. "You start making trouble for me and I'll tell Haley about the time Mom walked in on you with those two cheerleaders. If I remember correctly the three of you were naked."

Kevin winced. "I was only sixteen," he protested. "I didn't know what I was doing."

"You seemed to know exactly what you were doing. As for being sixteen, that doesn't help your cause. The cheerleaders were both in college."

Kevin grumbled under his breath, then nodded his

agreement. "I won't make trouble with Stephanie," he promised.

Nash believed him. Kevin had never wasted his time with lies.

He knew Kevin thought he was doing Nash a favor by wanting things to work out with Stephanie. What Kevin didn't know was Nash wrestled with more than a bad marriage. His brother knew how Tina had died, but not the details. She'd been killed in the line of duty. What Kevin didn't know was that she'd been assigned as backup on one of Nash's negotiations.

His superiors had never blamed him, but Nash knew what had really happened that day. He'd been responsible for the death of his wife as surely as if he'd detonated the bomb himself.

## Chapter Ten

Nash put his arm around Stephanie and drew her close. She leaned her head against his shoulder and sighed. The soft puff of air teased his neck and made him think of other ways they could be touching. The blood heating in his body told him to get her upstairs right that second, but he resisted the desire growing inside him. They had the whole night to make love. Right now he was enjoying being next to her.

The night was clear and cool. Overhead, stars glittered in the sky. He could hear the faint sound of a stereo next door. The boys were in bed, but probably not asleep yet, which was another reason to wait before heading inside.

"What are you thinking?" Stephanie asked from her seat next to him on the top step of the porch. "That you're so incredibly hot for my body that you're tempted to rip off my clothes right here? And if that's not what you're thinking, you need to lie.''

Nash smiled. ''I was also thinking about your kids, that it would be better to wait until the little guys are asleep, then head inside.''

''Good point. As long as you were thinking about it.''

He turned his head and brushed his lips against her forehead. ''I'm having trouble thinking about anything else.''

''An excellent quality in a man.'' She wrapped her arms around his waist. ''Dinner was fun. Thanks for joining us.''

''I had a good time, too. The twins look so much alike, yet their personalities are different enough that I don't have any trouble telling them apart.''

''I know. I don't understand how they can be so physically identical and so unalike on the inside. I've always wondered if some personality gene didn't split exactly in half or something.''

He grinned. ''That would be your technical, bio-chemical explanation?''

''Do you have a better one?''

''No. Yours is perfect.''

She laughed. ''I'm a fairly intellectual person, which explains why I beat your fanny when we were playing Go Fish.''

''You are a card shark.''

She winced. ''Bad pun, but I forgive you. The whole evening was fun. Sometimes I get so caught up with the boys' homework schedules and their activities that I forget to take time for us to just hang out and enjoy each other's company. Life becomes a treadmill and the routine becomes all-important.

Occasionally I need a reminder that it's okay to have a good time. Thanks for doing that tonight.''

"My pleasure." He dropped his hand to her hip and rubbed the curve there. "You said something earlier that I can't stop thinking about."

"What?" She raised her head and looked at him.

"You wanted to know why men refused to stop acting like little boys. The implication being we don't grow up. I know you were teasing when you said it, but I wonder if that's what you really believe."

She pulled back slightly, shifting so she faced him. One of her hands rested on his knee, the other toyed with the sleeve hem of his shirt. In the porch light, he could see her large eyes and the way the corners of her mouth twisted slightly.

"You're the first man I've ever spent any time with who seems to be a grown-up," she said. "My father was completely irresponsible and I've told you about the horror of being married to Marty. I've been burned twice and that makes me less than trusting."

"Is that the real reason you haven't been dating?"

"Yikes! Talk about going for the throat."

"Is it?"

"Maybe. Probably. I don't know."

"Come on." He put his hand over hers and squeezed. "You do know."

Her gaze narrowed. "You have that masters in psychology, don't you? Now you want to try out some of your theories on me."

"You're avoiding the question."

"And doing a fine job if it, too. Okay." She nodded. "I'll be serious. Yes, avoiding boys disguised as men is one of the reasons I haven't been very excited about dating. I have three kids and no time to raise a fourth. You seem decent and normal, but this is a part-time fling, not something serious. With my past, I think I have the right to be wary.''

He understood her point, but didn't like the idea of her spending the rest of her life alone. He was about to say so when he realized he didn't especially like the idea of her with someone else, either.

That made him slam on the mental brakes. No way was he thinking about anything serious with Stephanie. She was strictly temporary.

''At some point you have to be willing to take a chance,'' he said.

''Why? What are the odds that I'll end up with someone exactly like Marty? I seem to be destined to head in that direction. He was the first guy I really fell for. I don't want to risk it again.''

''So take it slow this time. Really get to know the guy.''

''The way I got to know you? Despite my claim of being responsible, I seem to be a bit impulsive in the relationship department.'' She laughed. ''Trust me. This is much better. I'm having a great time with you and right now that's enough. I have no interest in getting married again.''

They had that in common, he thought. Even though she was saying all the right things, he couldn't help worrying about her. ''What about money?''

Her eyes widened. ''Gee, Nash, the sex was really great, but I never planned to pay you for it.''

''That's not what I meant.''

She shimmied close. ''But now that we're on the

subject, I think I'm good enough that you should pay me.''

He laughed and hauled her onto his lap. ''Do you?''

''Uh-huh.''

She straddled him, her heat pressing against his suddenly hard arousal. She rocked back and forth, teasing them both.

''That feels nice,'' she said. ''And big. Is all that for little ol' me?'' Her voice was a soft purr.

''Think you can handle it?''

''There's nothing I want to do more than handle all of you. Let's go inside and get naked.''

Her words set him on fire. While he wanted to take her at her word, he couldn't help holding back long enough to kiss her. Her mouth parted instantly and he plunged inside her. She stroked against him, then clamped her lips around his tongue and sucked until he thought he might lose it right there. So much for having control.

He shifted her off his lap and scrambled to his feet. When he'd pulled her into a standing position, he wrapped his arms around her and lifted until her feet were dangling. She wrapped her legs around his hips and hung on. He started toward the front door.

''I want to tell you that I can walk,'' she murmured between kisses, ''but this is so much more exciting.''

''For me, too.'' He cupped her rear, holding her firmly against his erection. ''Besides, doesn't every woman want to be swept away?''

''Honey, you're doing that in spades.''

Under any other circumstances, Stephanie would have assumed that breaking into song while dusting the main parlor was reason to think about seeing a mental health professional. It was the middle of the afternoon and she wasn't even listening to the radio. But she decided to cut herself some slack. After all, she hadn't slept the previous night. Instead of wasting seven or eight hours with her eyes closed, she'd spent them in Nash's arms where she discovered that women did indeed hit their sexual peak in their thirties. While she was more than a little tired, she figured she could catch up on her rest when Nash was gone. Far better to take advantage of his proximity, interest and skill while he was in town.

She stretched up to dust the top of a lamp and the muscles in her back pulled slightly. She smiled as she remembered the shower they'd taken that morning. How she'd gripped the shower door frame to keep from falling as he'd knelt between her legs. The hot water had poured over both of them as he'd used his tongue to make her scream and shudder and go all weak at the knees…literally.

Still humming a somewhat embarrassing medley of tunes from cartoons, she finished in the parlor and walked toward the kitchen. She had to figure out what they were having for dinner. Then maybe they'd all head over to the video store and rent a couple of movies. School was out tomorrow and none of the boys had any homework. They could—

The sound of voices interrupted her thoughts. She paused to figure out where they were coming from. She recognized Nash's low rumble and the twins, but where on earth could they be? She tilted her head. The utility room?

Following the sound, she walked through to the

rear of the house. Sure enough, Nash crouched in front of Adam and Jason in the laundry. Between them sat an overflowing laundry basket.

Stephanie knew exactly what was going on. She'd told the twins to take the laundry upstairs and fold it. For the most part they were willing to do their chores, but laundry was the one thing all three of the boys hated more than just about anything.

No one noticed her standing in the doorway. As she watched, Nash touched each boy on the shoulder.

"You have a responsibility to your family," he said. "Your mom works hard to provide for you. In return, you go to school and help out when asked. Do you understand?"

Both boys nodded.

Nash smiled. "Good. If you work together as a team, the job will go that much quicker. Agreed?"

Two more nods, followed by Jason saying, "But Adam's gotta fold the laundry. I did it last time."

Adam turned on his twin. "You did not. I did it. It's your turn. You're always trying to get me to do your chores and I'm not gonna do this one."

"So this is an ongoing dispute," Nash said calmly. "How do you keep track of whose turn it is?"

Jason drew his eyebrows together. "It's his turn."

"Is not."

"So there's nothing in writing," Nash said.

Both boys shook their head. Their mouths were set in straight, stubborn lines and they had their arms folded over their chests.

"Why don't we talk about negotiating a system

that would be fair to both of you,'' Nash said reasonably.

Stephanie held in a laugh. It all sounded really good, but these were eight-year-olds. If Nash didn't come to his senses, he was going to be talking for the next three days and would probably end up folding the laundry himself out of self defense.

She stepped into the room and pointed at the laundry basket.

"Take that upstairs,'' she said firmly. "Now. You each fold half the clothes in that basket. If there is an uneven number of clothes, leave the last one on your bed. If you don't start upstairs right this instant, there will be no dessert for either of you.''

Jason opened his mouth to protest. She stopped him with a shake of her head.

"Not one word,'' she said. "One word means you're in bed ten minutes early. Two words means twenty minutes early. If you understand and agree, then nod slowly.''

Both boys looked at her, then at each other. They sighed heavily and nodded.

"Good.'' She stepped back to give them room to carry out the basket. "Come let me know when you're done.''

They each grabbed a handle and carried the basket into the hallway. Nash watched them go.

"I'm a professional,'' he said.

"You work with criminals. These are young boys. I'm going to guess that criminals are a lot more rational.''

"You think?''

She smiled. "I would put money on it. But thanks for helping. I really liked what you said about them having responsibilities. I'm not sure it sunk in, but maybe next time.''

He wrapped an arm around her shoulders. ''You're saying I stink at parenting.''

''I'm saying you're a sweetie to try.''

He tugged on a strand of her hair, then released her. ''Give me your car keys.''

''They're upstairs on the table by the door to our apartment. Why? Is your rental acting up?''

''No. I want to put gas in your car. Mind if I go get the keys?''

She nodded because it was suddenly too difficult to speak. Okay, in the scheme of things, Nash putting gas in her car was no big deal. But the unexpected thoughtfulness made her throat get all tight and her eyes burn. As he walked to the stairs, she found herself wishing—just for a second—that he wasn't leaving in a week or so. That his stay in Glenwood might be a little more permanent.

''Crazy dreams,'' she whispered. ''You know better.''

The phone rang, offering a welcome interruption. She headed for the kitchen and grabbed the receiver.

''Serenity House. This is Stephanie.''

''Hi, Stephanie. It's Rebecca Lucas. We met at that pizza dinner a couple of nights ago. I don't know if you remember me. There were so many people there.''

Stephanie pictured a tall, slender woman with long, dark curly hair. ''Yes, of course I remember. How are you?''

''Good. The reason I'm calling is Jill just called me. Craig—he's the oldest Haynes' brother—got the evening off. His kids are out of school today.

They're in a different school district. Anyway, we're celebrating with an impromptu barbecue here tonight. I think all of Nash's brothers will be coming and I wanted to invite him." She laughed. "Actually I want to invite you and your boys, as well, if that's all right."

Stephanie knew Nash didn't have any plans and she was pretty sure he wouldn't mind the invitation. She hesitated before accepting for all of them. Was that too presumptuous? Then she remembered his request that she help him out with his family.

"I'm sure it is, but let me double-check with him. Hold on just a sec."

She put the phone on the counter and moved toward the stairs. She met Nash as he was coming down and explained about Rebecca's phone call.

"You want to go?" he asked.

"Yes, but they're your family. Do *you* want to go?"

"As long as you're coming, sure."

"Good. I know the boys will enjoy the evening."

She took a step back, but couldn't seem to look away from Nash's dark gaze. Just being close to him was enough to get her heart all fluttery and her toes curling. Attraction crackled between them and she swayed slightly.

"Yeah," he said. "Me, too. Now go back to your phone call. Going out will make the evening go faster. When we get home, it will be time for the boys to go to bed."

Her stomach clenched. "Then us, too," she whispered.

"My thoughts exactly."

* * *

Stephanie carried a plastic freezer bag full of chocolate chip cookies up to the back door of the huge house. She hesitated slightly before entering. While she remembered meeting Rebecca Lucas at the pizza dinner, she and the woman weren't friends. Just walking into the house seemed rude, but knocking when there were kids running in and out seemed weird.

Before she could decide what to do, Rebecca pushed open the door and smiled.

"I saw you walking up from your minivan," she said easily. "You lost the kids in the first five feet and Kyle came to claim Nash. Let me help you with those." She took the bag of cookies from Stephanie. "We'll appreciate these."

"You said I didn't need to bring anything, but I wasn't comfortable coming empty-handed. They're still frozen if you want to pop them in the freezer. They'll keep well for another few weeks."

"Not a chance." Rebecca led the way to an oversize blue-and-white kitchen with gleaming stainless-steel appliances. "Between our kids and the Haynes kids and friends popping in, the cookies won't last two days."

She set the bag on the counter and turned to Stephanie. "The men are out getting the coals ready and all the salads are in the refrigerator. So there's not much for us to do right now but relax. May I get you something to drink?"

"Sure. Iced tea if you have it."

"Have a seat."

Rebecca waved toward several bar stools at the end of the counter. Stephanie took a seat as her hostess poured her a glass of iced tea.

"Jill's upstairs with the little ones. I think she's reading a story. Elizabeth, Holly and Sandy are outside supervising the play area. Kevin, Gage and their fiancées haven't arrived yet." Rebecca laughed. "Oh, dear. I should probably pull out the name tags. This is going to be a muddle."

Stephanie shook her head. "I'm pretty sure I have everyone figured out. What I don't know I can fake."

"Always a good plan."

Rebecca leaned against the counter. Her long curly hair tumbled down her shoulders. She wore a calf-length pale blue dress patterned with tiny white and pink flowers. There didn't seem to be any makeup on her flawless skin. She was tall, slender, lovely and looked as if she belonged in the pages of a Jane Austen novel.

"We were all very curious about you," Rebecca admitted. "Kevin swore his brother wasn't seeing anyone."

Stephanie hadn't expected that line of questioning. She'd picked up her glass, but now she put it down and folded her hands onto her lap. "We're not exactly seeing each other."

They were, she supposed. After a fashion. Seeing each other naked. But that was different. Rebecca was talking about an actual relationship.

"I'm not sure I believe you," Rebecca said. "I saw the way he was looking at you the other night." She held up her hands. "I'm not going to say any more about it. My goal isn't to torment you. When I first heard about Nash I thought he might be someone I could introduce to my friend, D.J. I don't think that's such a good idea now."

Stephanie felt as neatly trapped as a goldfish in a glass bowl. So how exactly was she supposed to respond to Rebecca's statement? There was no way she wanted Nash involved with someone else—it would cut into their affair time. There was also a hint of discomfort at the thought of him with another woman, but there was no way she was about to explore that particular emotion.

"Nash and I are friends," she said at last. "He's only in town for a couple of weeks, so *your* friend is unlikely to find him anything but temporary."

"How long does it take to fall in love?" Rebecca asked. "You might just be friends now, but that could change."

Stephanie reached for her glass. "No way. I'm smarter than that."

Rebecca raised her eyebrows. "You not a fan of marriage?"

"It's great for a lot of people."

"Just not you."

"Something like that."

Rebecca's expression turned dreamy. "I can't imagine not being married to Austin. He and the children are my entire world. I suppose that sounds silly and old-fashioned. I have a job, although I'm only working part-time these days. I have friends. But all of that pales next to what I feel for my husband."

Stephanie was surprised by a stab of envy. "That sounds lovely," she said. "My marriage wasn't exactly like that."

"Haynes men make excellent husbands," Rebecca told her. "Austin is an honorary Haynes. Nash is one, too. He's—"

But she never got to finish saying what Nash was. Several small children burst into the kitchen, followed by a petite redhead Stephanie recognized.

"Hi, Jill," she said as the other woman approached.

"Stephanie. I heard you and Nash were joining us. That's great." She bent down when a little girl of three or four pulled on her jeans. "Sarah, I told you we're not going to have a snack. We'll be eating in about half an hour. But I will get you something to drink."

Two more children of about the same age also clamored for drinks. Rebecca agreed. After opening a cupboard, she pulled out stacks of small plastic glasses and put them on the counter.

"We have juice and milk and chocolate milk," she said.

Everyone wanted something different. Rebecca poured while Jill passed out the half-full glasses.

Stephanie found herself the odd man out and crossed to the large window overlooking the massive backyard. More children were playing on a built-in play set. Older kids sat in groups talking. She could see all the Haynes men talking together around the big barbecue pit, while their wives had pulled plastic chairs under a tree. Everyone seemed to be having a good time.

What a great family, she thought. Growing up, she would have given anything to belong to a group like this. Being the only child of parents more interested in art than real life had given her plenty of time on her own to wish for friends and cousins and family.

She returned her attention to the men. Elizabeth

came up and stood next to Travis. He smiled at his wife and put his arm around her. Even from across the lawn, Stephanie could see the love in his eyes. Rebecca was right—Haynes men did seem to make good husbands. There didn't seem to be one like Marty in the bunch.

She studied each of them in turn, finally settling her gaze on Nash. He stood a little off to one side. In that instant, he appeared so alone that her heart squeezed tight. She wanted to go to him, hold him close and—

And what? He was leaving, remember?

For the first time, that information didn't make her happy.

She started to turn away from the window when she caught sight of Jason running toward Nash. Her eight-year-old flung out his arms and launched himself. Nash caught him easily. Man and boy laughed together. Stephanie felt her mouth curve up in response.

She pressed her fingers against the glass, as if she could touch them both. Longing filled her. A longing that was foolish and dangerous. Caring wasn't an option, she reminded herself. She and Nash had set down very clear rules and it was way too late to think about breaking them. It was also pointless. Even if she was crazy enough even to consider having a change of heart, Nash wasn't. Something she was going to have to remember.

## Chapter Eleven

After dinner the men collected the trash and cleaned up the picnic area while the women and kids disappeared inside the house to take care of dessert. Nash pulled a beer out of the cooler and passed it to Craig, then took one for himself.

All the brothers were sprawled out on chairs around the cooling fire pit. Jordan leaned forward with his forearms on his knees.

"You're jealous because I wasn't afraid to be a rebel," he said.

Travis grinned. "Yeah, right, because only a really smart guy runs into a burning building. Are you crazy?"

"If he is, we probably all are," Kyle joked, then turned to Nash. "You've heard about our black-sheep brother here, right? The only non-law enforcement officer in four generations of Haynes men.

Hell, even Hannah works for the sheriff's office. But did Jordan pay attention to all those years of tradition?''

''Not for a second,'' Jordan said cheerfully.

Nash glanced at Kevin. ''Four generations of Haynes men?'' he asked. He and Kevin hadn't considered other relatives beyond the half brothers and their families.

''Not all living,'' Craig clarified. ''We have a few uncles still in the area, but we don't see them very often.''

Nash watched as the four Haynes brothers exchanged a look of silent communication. Before he could ask what they were talking about, Travis nodded, then began to explain.

''Our uncles are a lot like our father. They never much believed in home and family. They think it's all a waste of time. Now that we're all happily married, they consider us sell-outs.''

''Why?'' Nash asked. ''Didn't they want you to get married?''

''No. They like women. A lot of women. Earl Haynes, our father, was the only one of his brothers to get married. I doubt he was faithful a day in his life. He used to brag that he was a good husband and father because he came home every night. In his mind sleeping in his own bed was good enough. Who he'd been with before that didn't seem to matter.''

''They used to fight,'' Kyle said quietly. ''I would hear them yelling at each other. She would beg him to stop seeing the other women and he would laugh at her. Then one day she left.''

''What do you mean, left?'' Kevin asked.

"She disappeared," Jordan said. "It turns out Earl asked her for a divorce. After all she'd already been through she considered that the final straw. She took off and no one has heard from her since."

Once again the brothers shared a look of silent communication, then Travis spoke.

"About three years ago our wives got together and organized a family meeting. They insisted we find out what happened to her. We hired a private investigator to track her down."

"She's fine," Travis said. "Living in Phoenix. She didn't remarry, but she's involved with someone who makes her happy."

"What did she say when you got in touch with her?" Kevin asked.

"We didn't," Craig told him. "We know she's all right. If she wanted to talk to any of us, she would know where to find us."

Kyle took a long drink of his beer. "It's not her fault," he said. "After years of dealing with Earl, she's paid her dues. She doesn't want anything to do with Haynes men and who can blame her?"

Nash understood the logic, but he wasn't sure he agreed with it. The sons were very different from the father. But if she'd left without a word…he could see why they wouldn't want to be the ones to make the first move.

"What is biology and what isn't?" Austin asked, speaking for the first time. "None of us have figured that out."

"True enough," Travis said. "How much of our father makes us who we are? Why, after three generations of womanizers, did my brothers and I finally figure out how to have successful relationships?"

"It wasn't easy," Craig said. "I made a mistake my first time out and I have the divorce to prove it."

"Me, too," Travis said. "But once I met Elizabeth, everything fell into place."

Jordan looked toward the house. "Finding the right woman makes all the difference in the world."

"I know that," Kevin said with a conviction Nash envied. After years of playing the field, of never wanting to settle down, he'd finally fallen in love.

Nash suddenly wanted to ask them how they knew for sure. How could any one woman be the right one? When he and Tina had been dating he'd never thought of her as right or wrong. She was someone he was seeing. When she'd pushed to take things to the next level, he'd agreed. When she'd demanded marriage, he'd considered his options and had finally proposed. But had she been the right one? He doubted it.

"Now we're old boring married men," Craig said. "Kids, mortgages, steady jobs and great wives."

Travis held up his beer. "Here's to not changing a thing."

The men clinked cans. Nash joined in, but he knew he didn't have anything to toast. Did he want his life to stay exactly the same? Two weeks ago he would have said yes, that he had all he wanted. Now, after spending time with Stephanie, he wasn't so sure. She'd reminded him that there was more to living than simply showing up every day. Participation was required, and he'd been going out of his way to avoid that.

The back door of the house opened and dozens of kids spilled out onto the lawn. The women followed, several holding cakes, others with plates of cookies or cartons of ice cream. Stephanie had plates, forks and spoons in her hands.

He watched her move, watched the easy way she walked and how she smiled when Adam and Jason came running up. She bent down and said something to them. They laughed, responded, then turned toward him.

Adam spotted him first. He pointed and the twins raced toward him. He had just enough time to set his can of beer on the grass, out of harm's way before both boys plowed into him. Jason hung on to one leg while Adam wrapped his arms around his neck.

"Mom said we can have ice cream with our cake," Jason announced with glee.

Adam ducked his head. "She said I could have a corner piece. Are you having cake, Nash?"

"Absolutely."

"Then come on."

Each twin grabbed a hand and tried to pull him to his feet. He shifted his weight and stood. As he glanced over their heads he saw Kevin watching him. His brother's expression was knowing.

Nash wanted to stop and say something. That whatever Kevin was thinking, he was wrong. Nash didn't have it bad—he didn't have it at all. This time with Stephanie was a pleasant distraction, but little else. It couldn't be more…not when he considered the price he would pay for taking another chance on getting involved.

The boys didn't settle down immediately. It took three tries and several threats to finally get them into bed and the lights off. Stephanie closed Brett's door and headed for her living room where Nash was waiting for her. She sank down next to him on the sofa.

"We're going to have to give it a little time," she said. "I'm pretty sure they're down for the night, but they may take a while to fall asleep."

"So we'll talk until they do."

She angled toward him so she could stare at his handsome face. "Halfway decent in bed and he likes to talk," she teased. "How did I get so lucky?"

"It's a question you must ask yourself every morning."

She laughed. "Surprisingly I have other things on my mind when I get up."

"I am surprised. You shouldn't be thinking about anything but how good I make you feel."

Actually that was the first thing on her mind, but she wasn't about to admit that to him. Not when he was already so confident about his abilities in the bedroom. Not that he had reason to be anything but impressed with himself. Lord knows he made her entire being tingle.

"I had a good time tonight," she said. "You have a great family."

"I agree. I still have trouble believing they've been out there all this time, and I never knew about them."

"I used to dream about finding out I had a big

family,'' she admitted. ''I wanted aunts and uncles and lots and lots of cousins. Especially at the holidays. It was always really quiet at our house. My parents surfaced from their work enough to remember it was Christmas or my birthday, but they never really participated. I remember they used to give me board games as presents, but then never take the time to play with me. I used to try playing both sides myself, but it wasn't very much fun.''

Nash's eyes darkened. ''That's sad.''

She held up a hand. ''Don't look stricken. I recovered. I'm just saying more kids around would have been really nice. At least you always had Kevin.''

''Not just him, but Gage and Quinn, too. We were always over at each other's houses. Gage, Kevin and I are the same age and Quinn is only a year younger, so we hung out all the time. Our moms were friends, as well.'' He leaned his head back on the sofa cushion. ''We used to say we were like brothers. Ironically, that turned out to be true.''

''Where is the mysterious Quinn?'' she asked. ''I keep hearing about him, but I've yet to see him.''

''He works for the government. Some secret branch of the military. His work takes him around the world and he's not always accessible. Gage left a message and as soon as he gets it, he'll show up.''

''He sounds a little dangerous. Why am I picturing a guy all in black and carrying really big guns.''

''I don't know, but that sounds like Quinn.''

She shivered. ''Not my kind of guy. Was he scary when you were growing up?''

''Not scary, but a bit of an outsider. He and his dad didn't get along.'' Nash frowned. ''I guess

Ralph isn't really his father anymore. Not biologically.'' He looked at her. ''Ralph and Edie couldn't have kids of their own. It's a complicated story.''

''I think it's great that their mom helped out your mom when she was abandoned by her own family. Even if you and your brother didn't know you were related to Gage and Quinn, you still got to grow up as close friends.''

''I'm glad Edie was a caring person. My mom was in a hell of a bad situation.'' He shook his head. ''Barely eighteen, with babies. What kind of parents would throw their daughter out of the house under those conditions? Edie was really there for her.''

He reached out and covered her hand with his. ''Who's there for you, Stephanie?''

The question surprised her. ''I have friends. In a pinch they would come through.''

''What about on a day-to-day basis?''

''Unfortunately there aren't a lot of people lining up to play second string,'' she admitted. ''But I do okay.''

''Is okay good enough?''

This line of conversation could lead to very dangerous territory, she thought. Dangerous and tempting. While she might not mind fantasizing about Nash stepping in to provide backup, reality was very different, and she had to remember to keep the two worlds separate.

''Hard question to answer, as I don't have a choice in the matter.'' She squeezed his fingers. ''Hey, let's change the subject. Your entire responsibility for me consists of pleasing me in bed. Nothing more.''

He studied her as if he wanted to say more, then nodded.

"They were talking about our father tonight," he said. "Earl Haynes was something of a bastard."

"I've heard bits of gossip over the past few years."

"He slept around and didn't seem to care about his wife or sons. All the brothers worry that they'll turn out like him."

"From what I've seen, none of them have. Are you worried, too?"

He shrugged.

She leaned close. "You can let that one go."

"Why? How do you know I'm different? I'm sleeping with you."

"Yes, but that's simply proof of your excellent taste."

The corners of his mouth curved up. "You think?"

"I know."

They were close enough that she could inhale the scent of him and feel his heat. Wanting flooded her, but she didn't act on the need. Part of it was she wanted to give the boys a few more minutes to fall asleep, and part of it was how much she liked the anticipation. After so many years of chaste living, it was fun to suddenly feel like a sex kitten.

"Having the information about your father means that you get to make informed choices," she said. "You know what to look out for."

"One of your choices was staying with Marty," he said. "Was it a good one?"

She sighed. "As far as my sons are concerned, yes. I wouldn't give them up for anything. But as far as making me personally happy in my marriage, no. Marty wasn't a good choice.''

He reached out and stroked her cheek. ''Are you okay? Financially?''

''Didn't we already have this conversation?'' she asked.

''Yes and you didn't answer the question.''

''Let me guess. You're not going to let it go until I do, right?''

He nodded.

She knew she could shut him down by pointing out that none of this was his business. But Nash wasn't asking out of anything but concern. Although she had no clue what he would do if he thought she was in need. Offer her a low-interest loan?

The thought was mildly amusing, but not much of a distraction. Was she going to tell him the truth or not?

She settled on the truth because she'd never been a very good liar.

''We're doing okay,'' she said slowly. ''I've told you what life was like with Marty so you know that there wasn't a lot of extra cash each month. I held down the only steady job in the family, so that made things tight. When Marty got the inheritance, it seemed like a miracle.''

''I was surprised when you told me he'd agreed to buy a house. It doesn't sound like his style.''

''Oh, it wasn't. We had huge fights. In the end, he gave in, but with a twist. We bought this place instead of a regular single-family home.''

She glanced around at the high ceilings of her third-floor living area. ''At first I hated it. The last thing I wanted was a big mortgage and a lot of remodeling. When Marty died, I was furious. I'd been left with this disaster. But over time, I realized it was the best thing that could have happened. We get a lot of tourists up here, and many of them love the idea of staying at a bed and breakfast. I've been able to do most of the remodeling myself, which has saved a lot of money. I make my own schedule, and I'm here when the boys get home from school. A regular job would mean day care and that would be financially impossible.''

''Interesting information,'' he said, ''but you haven't answered the question.''

''We do okay,'' she told him. ''Some months are tight, some aren't. I did manage to keep a small life insurance policy up on Marty so when he died there was some money from that. I put it away. If push comes to shove, it's my emergency fund. Fingers crossed I never have to use it.'' She held up one hand.

''If all goes well,'' she continued, ''I'll use it to pay for the boys' college. So I'm fine. Really.''

He smiled. ''You're more than fine. You're responsible, giving and a great mom.''

His compliment pleased her, which she told herself was silly. Still, she sat a little straighter and fought the urge to beam.

''I try.''

''You succeed.''

She shifted and, still facing him, leaned against the back of the sofa. ''Okay, fair's fair. You got to ask me a very personal question and now I get to do the same.''

''All right.''

She thought about all the possibilities and settled on the one that troubled her the most.

"Tell me about your wife."

She watched closely, but Nash's expression didn't change. "What do you want to know?"

"Whatever you want to tell me. Whatever…"

Her voice trailed off as a horrifying thought occurred to her. Did he not want to talk about the woman because she still mattered so much? He'd claimed not to be thinking about her when they made love, but what if he'd been lying? What if there were ghosts who—

"That's not the reason," he said.

She blinked at him. "What are you talking about?"

"I'm hedging because I don't know what to say about her, not because I'm heartbroken."

"That's a relief." She pressed her lips together. "Wait a minute. How did you know what I was thinking?"

"It was a logical assumption."

"Uh-huh."

She didn't buy that for a second. But what other explanation could there be? How strange that Nash knew her so well after just a short period of time, and despite all their years together, Marty had never known her at all. Was Marty's lack of knowledge due to some flaw within him, or had he never found her all that interesting?

"When I started working for the FBI," he said, "I quickly learned that emotional detachment was an asset. Nearly every situation is difficult on some level and leading with your heart is a good way to make the wrong decision. Staying emotionally distant was something I'd learned while I was growing up and it served me well at the bureau.''

Having heard about his close family, Stephanie couldn't imagine how or why Nash would detach. Sometimes he seemed a little distant with his family, but that could have been shyness or emotional reserve. Nothing about his relationship with her and her kids indicated he was anything but emotionally available, but this wasn't the time to go into that particular subject. She filed the question away to spring on him later.

''I've told you a bit about Tina. She was my opposite. Emotional, disorganized, leading with her heart instead of her head. I wasn't even sure I liked her at first.'' His gaze narrowed slightly. ''I'm talking about after she was an agent. I never considered her as anything but a co-worker during training.''

''Of course not,'' she murmured, believing him. Nash would never break that kind of rule.

''Dating led to more dating. After a while Tina suggested we live together. Marriage seemed like the next logical step.''

How interesting, she thought. Had Tina been the one guiding the relationship? Nash almost made it sound like he was only along for the ride.

''How old were you when you got married?'' she asked.

''Twenty-seven.''

Okay—the right age for most guys to think about settling down. So had Tina been in the right place at the right time? Not a question she would be asking.

Stephanie resisted the urge to slap herself upside the head. She knew exactly what she was doing. If she could convince herself to believe Nash had married Tina because it was "time" and not because he was wildly in love with her, somehow that would make Stephanie feel better about their relationship. Crazy but true. She told herself to get over it.

"You didn't have a chance to have kids," she said. "I guess she passed away before you got around to that."

He shrugged. "We never talked about it. I always wanted children. I guess Tina did, too. Then she was killed."

"How?" she asked before she could stop herself.

"In the line of duty. A bomb exploded."

She'd been expecting a lot of answers, just not that one. A bomb sounded so violent. Because it *was* violent, she thought. Violent and unexpected and shocking.

"I'm sorry," she whispered.

"Thanks."

Nash's expression hadn't changed as he talked, but there was something in his eyes that tugged at her heart.

"Want to talk about this more or change the subject?" she asked.

"Let's move on."

"Okay. So how did a guy with a twin brother and close friends learn to disconnect emotionally while he was growing up?" she asked.

He shook his head. "Easier than you might think. My mom married a guy when Kevin and I were twelve. Howard and I never got along."

That surprised her. "Still? But he and your mother are expected the day after tomorrow. Is that going to be a problem?" She frowned. "Why on earth did you want them staying here if you two aren't speaking?''

"We're speaking. And we get along."

The words sounded right, but she wasn't sure she believed them. "You're not going to be yelling at each other in the foyer, are you?"

"No. If there's any yelling, we'll do it outside where it belongs."

She smiled. "Fair enough. So is this emotional detachment you're so fond of the reason you haven't gotten involved with anyone else since your wife's death?"

"No. I've avoided relationships because I loved Tina and I can't ever love anyone else again."

Stephanie stared at him for several heartbeats, then burst out laughing. "Oh, come on. That's ridiculous. You can't love again? Did we move from real life to a TV soap? Are you saying the human heart is capable of only loving once? What about my three kids? Should I send the twins back because I already loved Brett when they arrived?"

Nash looked as shocked as if she'd pulled a gun on him. The charged silence between them made her wonder if she'd gone too far. He couldn't be serious about not loving again—people didn't work like that. But did he believe it? Had she just insulted him big-time?

She waited anxiously as he stared at her. She couldn't read his expression...not until one corner of his mouth twitched.

"You're not buying my best line?" he asked at last.

Relief swept through her. "Not for a second. Who has?"

"Everyone but you."

"I see. Are these 'everyones' women?"

"For the most part."

"Then you need to start dating women with slightly higher IQs."

He laughed and grabbed her around the waist, then hauled her onto his lap. "I prefer my women to have a little more respect than you do, Missy."

She settled her hands on his shoulders and brushed his mouth with hers. "That so isn't going to happen as long as you talk like an idiot."

"Idiot, huh? I'm one idiot you can't resist."

She leaned in to kiss him again. "You're right about that," she whispered and gave herself up to him.

## Chapter Twelve

"Batter up," Brett called, as he tossed the baseball in the air and caught it. "Adam, it's your turn."

Adam walked to the square marked on the grass in front of the house and clutched his bat. From what Nash could tell, Adam might be the quieter twin, but he was the better athlete. So far he'd been the one to hit the ball every time Brett pitched it.

Brett pitched a slow ball and Adam swung. There was a *crack* as the bat connected, then the ball flew directly back to Brett who had to jump to catch it.

"Good hit," he called to his brother.

Nash stood at the end of the porch, leaning against the house. The boys were playing in the side yard to, as Stephanie put it, "Avoid as many windows as possible."

The late-morning was warm and clear—the perfect weather for the start of summer vacation.

The boys had tumbled out of bed surprisingly early, apparently too excited by the thought of no school to sleep late. Stephanie had predicted their behavior, which meant she'd left his bed around four in the morning. He'd slept until he'd heard not-so-quiet footsteps on the stairs about quarter to seven. He was tired and his eyes felt gritty, but lack of sleep was a small price to pay for spending the night with a woman who defined female beauty and sexuality.

He quickly checked his thoughts, knowing that if he dwelled on all they'd done together while in bed, he would end up in a very uncomfortable state. It didn't seem to matter how many times they made love; he always wanted her more. Last night had been no different.

He heard the front door open, then the sound of footsteps on the porch.

"They should be here any minute," Stephanie said as she stopped beside him and leaned against the railing. She glanced at him. "Are you sure you're going to be okay with your mom and step-father staying here?"

He smiled. "I'm more than fine. I'm actually looking forward to their visit."

She didn't look convinced. "I would buy that a lot more easily if you hadn't told me you and your stepfather didn't get along."

"The problem's all on my side," Nash admitted, for the first time feeling comfortable with the truth. "Don't worry."

"I'll try not to." She turned toward the street, as if watching for cars. "If they're going to be staying here, we're going to have to be more careful about our sneaking around."

"Good point." One he hadn't considered.

She turned back to smile at him. "It will make things more exciting."

"I don't think that's possible. Not without one of us having a heart attack from the stress."

Her smile broadened. "Are you saying your affair with me is stressful?"

"I'm saying it's already more exciting than I thought possible. More excitement could be dangerous."

"But you're a big tough guy. Don't you live for danger?"

Her teasing words produced a predictable reaction. He ignored the sense of heat and heaviness flooding south. Good thing, too, because about eight seconds later a four-door sedan pulled up behind his rental car.

"They're here," he said.

Stephanie straightened. The humor faded from her eyes, replaced by worry. "Do I look okay?"

Despite the potential for an interested onlooker, he leaned forward and dropped a kiss on her mouth. "You look perfect."

Her expression cleared. "Excellent answer."

They walked to the porch steps, then onto the pathway. As they approached, the car doors opened. Nash's mother, Vivian, stepped out onto the sidewalk and smiled.

"What a lovely town. It's so charming. Nash, I swear, you're still getting taller."

He chuckled at the familiar claim, then folded her into his arms. "Hey, Mom. How was the trip?"

"Great." She kissed his cheek, then smoothed back his hair and rested her hands on his shoulders. "How are you?"

The question was about more than his state of being that day. He knew she wanted him to move on with his life, to let go of the past. To find someone else and settle down. He figured it was a "mom" thing.

"I'm good."

"Really?" Her gaze searched his face. "I hope so."

The car door slammed and she turned toward her husband. "Doesn't Nash look taller, Howard?"

"Viv, I'm going to guess our boy stopped growing a few years back," Howard said affectionately. He circled around the car and offered Nash his hand. As they shook, he patted Nash on the shoulder. "Good to see you. Life treating you well?"

"Always."

Nash stepped back and introduced Stephanie. "She owns Serenity House," he said. "You haven't lived until you've had her breakfasts."

"Nice to meet you, Mr. and Mrs. Harmon," she said. "I hope you'll enjoy your stay."

"Please call us Vivian and Howard," his mother said.

"Thank you."

There were a couple of yells from around the side of the house. Stephanie glanced in that direction. "I have three sons you'll meet later. While we live on the floor above your room, please don't worry. We're not directly overhead."

"We're going to have a lovely time," Vivian said, then tucked a strand of dark hair behind her ear. "How long have you had the bed and breakfast?" she asked.

"Almost four years. Would you like to see your room?"

"That would be nice."

Vivian turned to her husband. "Do you need me to carry anything in? I don't want you doing all the work."

Howard smiled at his wife. "I like taking care of you. Go on in and register. I'm sure Nash is going to insist on carrying the heaviest bag. We'll be fine."

Vivian nodded and touched Howard's arm. The contact wasn't anything special, just a brief brush of fingers, something Nash could remember having seen his mother do hundreds of times before. Yet for the first time, he saw the affection between the couple, the expression of happiness and contentment on his mother's face. She loved this man—she had for nearly twenty years.

The two women walked toward the house. Howard opened the trunk and laughed when he saw all the luggage. "Now you know why I had to rent a full-size car at the airport. Your mother isn't one to travel light. She always brings extras, just in case. I figure she packed enough for us to take a trip around the world, although she wouldn't agree. I guess if we ever did that, she'd want to bring the whole house. Just in case."

He shook his head, then started removing suitcases. Howard talked about the flight and who was looking in on their house while they were gone. As he spoke, Nash realized that there wasn't any strain between them. At least not on Howard's part.

They carried in the luggage and found Vivian and Stephanie by the registration desk.

"I was just telling your mother that the boys are pretty well behaved," Stephanie said. "There shouldn't be much noise."

Vivian shook her head. "And I was telling Stephanie that I miss the noise of having my boys in the house."

"I doubt that," Nash said. "You were always yelling at us to turn down the music or the TV or to stop revving our car engines in the driveway."

"Was I?" Vivian asked with a laugh. "I don't remember that at all."

"Would you like some lunch when you've unpacked?" Stephanie asked. "I don't have a restaurant here, but I would be delighted to make sandwiches, and I have several kinds of salad."

"That sounds lovely, dear," Vivian said. She linked arms with Stephanie. "Show me the way to the kitchen and I'll help while Howard and Nash take our things upstairs."

Stephanie looked a little startled by the suggestion. "You're a guest."

"Nonsense. I want to help. Or at least keep you company. You can tell me about your boys."

Stephanie glanced at Nash who gave her a smile. "You'll be fine," he said.

"Of course she will be," his mother said. "Now where's the kitchen?"

"Extra cheese on my sandwich," Howard called after them.

Vivian waved her fingers at him and laughed. "He always reminds me," she said as the two women turned down the hall. "As if I ever forget."

Nash picked up the key Stephanie had left on the desk and the two suitcases he'd brought in. "Ready to take these upstairs?" he asked.

"Lead the way."

They climbed to the second floor. Nash noticed right away that his room wasn't close to theirs, which meant he and Stephanie wouldn't have to tiptoe back and forth once everyone was in bed. Good planning on her part, he thought with a grin.

The room she'd chosen for them was large, with a king-size bed and a big bay window. Howard set his suitcases on the bed, took the ones Nash had carried and dropped them on the other side of the mattress.

"How are things going here?" Howard asked as he opened a garment bag and pulled out a suit, a sports coat and several dresses. "When Kevin called he said you two had already met your brothers."

"We've had a few group functions, as well as a lunch. When the whole Haynes family gets together, there are dozens of people. Everyone is married and has kids."

"Are they really all in law enforcement?"

"Except for Jordan. He's a firefighter."

Howard hung up the clothes. "Interesting. You and Kevin have followed in their footsteps. Gage and his brother, too." He returned to the bed and opened the largest suitcase. "Are they good men?"

Nash nodded. "Even the firefighter."

Howard chuckled. "Your mother worried about how things would go when you and Kevin arrived. Would the other brothers accept you two? Would you accept them? We're both glad it worked out." He scooped out toiletries and carried them into the bathroom. "We keep telling each other that you're grown up enough that we don't have to be concerned anymore, but maybe parents never let go of that."

Nash followed his stepfather into the bathroom. "You don't mean me," he said. "I wasn't the one getting into trouble."

Howard set two zippered cases on the counter. "True, but we wanted the best for you. You haven't been yourself for a while. I'm glad to see you getting back to normal."

He headed back to the bedroom and Nash followed. He knew that he'd been burying himself in his work, but he hadn't realized anyone but his boss had noticed.

"You mean because I'm finally taking a vacation?" he asked.

Howard shrugged. "That's part of it. Mostly you're smiling again. It's been a long time."

"Since Tina's death." Nash wasn't asking a question.

"No. The change happened before that." Howard picked up several shirts, then set them back in the suitcase and faced Nash. "There wasn't anything wrong with Tina. She was a perfectly nice young woman. But your mother and I never thought she was right for you. She was flighty and impulsive. Despite the parts of your job that force you to make split-second decisions, you're a thoughtful man. You consider your options. You use reason. Tina wasn't a good match for that."

Nash didn't know what to say. Howard's comments stunned him. Apparently Howard and his mother had thought his marriage to Tina was a mistake from the beginning, but they'd never said anything.

"Now Stephanie seems like a nice sort of woman," Howard said, resuming his unpacking. "It takes someone sensible to make a business successful. Vivian mentioned she's a widow. She was very young when her husband died."

The not-so-subtle matchmaking got Nash's attention. "Don't go there," he warned. "My stay here is temporary."

"You could move. You don't have any ties to Chicago." He smiled. "Okay, I'll be quiet. We don't care what you do, Nash, we just want you to be happy."

"Thanks. I appreciate that."

Howard mentioned something about how the Texas Rangers were doing that season. While Nash responded, he wasn't listening all that closely. Part of him was thinking about what the other man had said. About being happy. Nash couldn't remember the last time he could claim that. It had been well before Tina's death. Had it been before Tina?

Did it matter? Wasn't the more important point that he was happy now...maybe for the first time in years.

"I don't have enough plates," Stephanie said, trying not to panic. "Or glasses."

"Use plastic," Nash called as he walked through the utility room and out to the garage where there were several folding chairs.

"Use plastic," she muttered. "Easy for him to say." Although it was a pretty good idea. Did she have plastic?

She stopped in the center of the kitchen and tried to figure out if she'd stored any extra plastic glasses and plates after a birthday party for the twins. She dashed to a cupboard and pulled it open. Three unopened packages of plates sat on a top shelf she couldn't reach. At least she was making progress.

Nash returned with four chairs. "There are a couple more out there."

"We've brought down the chairs from upstairs, plus the ones in the dining room." She grimaced. "It's not nearly enough."

"Hey, stop sweating the details."

"You call having a place for people to sit a detail?"

"Sure. The kids will be happy on the ground." He put down the chairs and crossed to her. After resting his hands on her waist, he kissed her. "Thank you for offering to host the dinner."

Just being near him made her feel more calm. "I'm happy to have your family over. Really. But I need you to get those plates down for me."

When she took them from him, she happened to glance at her watch. The time made her shriek. "They're due back at any second. Get the chairs set up. I'll start stacking flatware."

Nash did as he was told and Stephanie raced to collect forks and spoons.

Kevin had called earlier to suggest another impromptu dinner for the family. Rather than cook, he'd offered to get Chinese. Stephanie had volunteered her place as the location. Vivian and Howard had taken the boys to meet Kevin and Haley at the Chinese restaurant, where they would buy enough

food to feed the army that was the extended Haynes/
Harmon/Reynolds family.

"Glasses," she murmured. "The sodas are already cooling in the big tub outside. I have milk and
juice for the kids. I made iced tea. There's a—"

A faint double ring caught her attention. She spun
in place. "Nash, your cell phone is ringing."

"Can you grab it?" he called from the utility
room. "It's on the front desk with my keys."

She ran to the front of the house. The ringing got
louder as she approached. When she saw the phone,
she picked it up and pressed Talk.

"Hello?"

There was a moment of silence before a man
asked, "I'd like to speak with Nash Harmon."

"Sure. Just a second."

She hurried into the hallway and found Nash carrying in more chairs. "It's for you," she said. "I'll
take those."

"They'll wait," he told her and leaned them
against the wall and reached for the phone.

She'd been about to politely retreat to the kitchen,
but he put his arm around her and drew her close.

"Harmon," he said into the phone.

She couldn't hear what the man was saying, so
she contented herself with relaxing against Nash's
strong, broad chest. She closed her eyes and
breathed deeply.

His chest rumbled as he spoke. "I thought you
didn't want me taking on any more assignments,"
he said.

After listening for a while longer he said, "I'll
think about it and get back to you." He chuckled.
"None of your business. Uh-huh. Yeah, she's gor-

geous. Tough luck. Get your own girl." A pause. "Okay. I'll let you know in a few days."

He hung up the phone.

"Your boss?" Stephanie asked, trying not to preen about the *Yeah, she's gorgeous* remark.

Nash nodded. "He wanted to tell me about a job opening up that I might be interested in. Different city, change of scene. He thought it would do me good."

She glanced at him. "Why do you need that?"

He tucked the phone into his shirt pocket and wrapped his other arm around her. "I didn't have a choice about my vacation. My boss insisted I take time off. He's been worried that I'm burning out."

That surprised her. "Why?"

"I haven't taken any time off since Tina died."

Stephanie's retreat was instinctive. Before she knew what she was doing, she'd pulled away far enough to lean against the opposite wall in the hall. She hated that Nash was no longer smiling.

"You're burying yourself in work?" she asked, knowing the question wasn't much of a stretch.

"Yeah, but not for reasons you think."

She didn't know *what* she thought. She only knew she didn't want him still to be in love with his late wife.

"Then what are the reasons?" she asked, careful to keep her voice neutral.

He sucked in a breath and stared at a spot well above her head. "I told you Tina was killed in the line of duty, by a bomb blast. What I didn't tell you is that I was there. I'd been called in to negotiate a hostage situation. I convinced the guys to give up. When they came out, I knew something wasn't right, but I couldn't figure out what. Later I realized things had gone too easily. I told the team to wait, but Tina didn't listen. She was her usual impulsive self. About ten seconds after she ran into the building to free the hostages, I found out why they'd given up."

Stephanie didn't want to think about it, didn't want to imagine it, but she knew what had happened. "The bomb went off."

He nodded, his face expressionless. "Tina, another agent and all the hostages were killed."

He blamed himself. She knew that because she knew Nash, and because under the same circumstances she might have blamed herself. Foolish, but true. "No one else thinks it's your fault."

He looked at her. "You don't know that."

"Am I wrong?"

"No."

"So you blame yourself and you bury yourself in work. Now your boss is offering a different job, thinking that the change will snap you out of it."

"Something like that."

"Do you need to be snapped out of it?"

His body relaxed. "Not right now. You're good for me, Stephanie."

His words warmed her in a way that had nothing to do with heat and everything to do with her heart. He was good for her, too. He made her want to believe in love and hope and the future. He made her want…

She mentally winced. No, don't go there, she told herself. Nash was temporary, remember? There was no point in wishing for the moon. She would only end up disappointed, with a crick in her neck.

"I aim to provide a full-service establishment,"

she said lightly. "Don't forget to mention all this on your comment card. It will impress the management."

He moved toward her. "I'm serious. Since I've met you—"

Whatever he'd been about to say got lost in the sound of car doors slamming. She was dying to know what he'd been about to say, but they were about to be invaded by the entire Haynes family.

"Save that thought," she told him even though she knew they would never discuss this topic again. She knew because she was going to make sure it never happened. Whatever Nash might want to tell her, it wasn't the one thing she wanted to hear. Namely that he'd decided to stay.

"I could never do what you do," Howard said the next morning.

"Most of my job is paperwork," Nash reminded him as they jogged through the quiet neighborhood.

"But when it isn't, there are lives on the line. I admire your ability to deal with that."

There was pride in Howard's voice as he spoke— a father's pride in his child. Nash realized he'd heard it dozens of times before. Maybe from the first time he'd met Howard. Hell, he thought, feeling like an idiot. He'd been so busy resenting his stepfather, he'd never noticed the man cared about him. Loved him.

"You had a hard time when you started dating Mom," Nash said. "I remember Kevin and I making things tough on you."

Howard grinned. "You made me work for my place," he said, his breathing slightly labored. "But it was worth it. Besides, I was crazy about your mother. A couple of my friends were worried that she was only interested in finding a father for you and your brother, but I loved her too much to care. Of course they were wrong. I guess nearly twenty years of marriage has proved that.''

They reached the corner and paused to check traffic before jogging across the street. The morning was clear and still a little cool, although it would warm up later.

''We were twelve when you two started going out,'' Nash said. ''If she'd wanted to find someone to be a father for us, she would have started looking earlier.''

Howard glanced at him, then wiped the sweat from his forehead. ''You were heading toward being teenagers. That's when boys really need a man around. Your mother worried about you.''

Howard had mentioned something similar the day before. ''Why me? I was the good kid.''

''Right. As the bad kid, Kevin got all the attention. Vivian was afraid you'd get forgotten in all the fuss. We talked about it a lot before we were married.''

Nash felt as if he'd missed out on most of what was going on while he'd been growing up. ''Why didn't I know about any of this?''

''You weren't supposed to. You were the child.''

They reached the edge of the middle-school playground and turned around.

Howard slowed to a walk. ''Whew. I'm not getting any younger.''

''You're still in great shape.''

Howard grinned. ''You're lying, but thanks. Anyway, Kevin continued to get into trouble and you continued to be the perfect child. When Kevin stole that car, we didn't know what to do. The police were the ones who suggested the military school. We figured they would probably be able to straighten him out and with Kevin gone, you'd have a chance to shine.''

Nash didn't think there were any more surprises to be had, but he'd been wrong. ''I didn't think you'd sent him away because of me,'' he said, oddly humbled by the information.

''Not because of you. Kevin was hell on wheels. But our concern about you swayed our decision.'' Howard slapped him on the back. ''You're both like my own sons. I would have loved Vivian as much without you two as part of the package, but just between us, knowing you boys came along with the deal made it irresistible.''

Nash didn't know what to say. He felt awkward and foolish. As if he'd been playing by one set of rules all these years, when there had been a completely different game in play.

''Howard,'' he began slowly. ''I—''

The older man smiled. ''I know, Nash. I've always known. I love you, too.''

In celebration of the kids all being out of school, the Haynes/Harmon/Reynolds family took over the large back room of the local pancake restaurant.

Nash sat at the big U-shaped table and listened to all the conversations flowing around him. In a crowd like this, his instinct was to withdraw—to observe rather than participate. But since his early-morning jog with his stepfather, he'd realized he'd better stop assuming anything about himself or his life. Apparently nothing was as he'd thought it had been.

All those years wasted, he thought sadly. Howard had been there for him and he'd never noticed. What else had he missed in his life?

The sound of laughter interrupted his thoughts. He looked across the table and saw Stephanie and Elizabeth laughing together. Petite, with short blond hair and a mouth designed specifically to drive him mad, Stephanie was a walking, breathing fantasy. He liked how she fit in with his family. In less than twenty-four hours she and his mother had become fast friends. She managed to keep his brothers, their spouses and kids straight.

He wanted her. That was hardly news, but the feeling this morning was different. He wanted more than sex. He wanted—

Nothing he was going to get, he reminded himself and looked away. He glanced around the table and saw Brett watching him. He smiled at the boy, who started to smile back, then instead turned away. Ironically, Nash knew exactly what the kid was thinking. He still saw Nash as a threat.

He thought about trying to reassure Brett again, but figured there wasn't any point. He, Nash, hadn't listened to Howard all those years ago. Why would Brett listen to him? Still he wished he had the right words. Life would be easier for Brett if he understood, just as life would have been a whole lot easier for Nash if he'd known that Howard wasn't a problem. All those wasted years when they could have been close.

He hated the regrets. The "could have beens." And he didn't just have them with Howard. What about his regrets with Tina? Their marriage had never been picture-perfect. Maybe if he'd worked harder to make it better. Maybe then he wouldn't feel so damn guilty all the time. Maybe—

His brain cleared. It was as if he'd been looking through a fog for the last two years, since the day of his wife's death.

Haltingly, almost afraid of what he would see, he looked at his brothers and their wives and fiancées. He looked at their faces, their eyes, and the way they were always touching. Husbands and wives in love with each other.

Love. That's what had been wrong with his marriage. He'd gone through the motions, but that's all it had been. He should never have married Tina because he'd never loved her. And it had taken him the better part of two years to figure that out.

## Chapter Thirteen

Stephanie watched the clock impatiently. It was 11:27. She and Nash had agreed she would head downstairs at 11:30. After some debate they'd decided it would be easier for her to explain her presence going up to her own floor than for him to say why he was heading down from hers.

In theory there was no reason to sneak. While it was best her children didn't know that she and Nash had become intimate, would it really matter to his parents? Not that she was going to suggest they spill the beans. In a way, having to wait heightened anticipation. She was already trembling slightly at the thought of seeing him and there was a definite heaviness low in her belly. One would think they had made love enough times for some of the thrill to be fading, but one would be wrong.

Two more minutes passed. At exactly 11:30, she

picked up her shoes, a travel alarm set for four in the morning and tiptoed out of her room. She made it down the hall to the stairs without making a sound then headed to the floor below.

At the third stair from the bottom, she stepped as close to the wall as possible to avoid the creaky step, then reached the second level and headed for Nash's room.

The door was already open. She stepped inside, prepared to remind him that she had to make it back to her own bed before anyone was stirring, but she wasn't given the opportunity to speak.

He'd been standing in the center of the room, just out of the pool of light given off by the bedside lamp. As she entered, he crossed to her and pulled her close. As his arms wrapped around her body, his mouth settled on hers. The deep, sensual, demanding kiss turned her bones to liquid.

She melted against him. Wanting flooded her, barely giving her enough time to drop her shoes and set the clock on the dresser. The door closed with a soft thud, then Nash's hands were everywhere—her back, her hips, her waist, her breasts.

They'd been together enough times that he knew what she liked, what she loved and what made her scream with delight, and he used that knowledge to reduce her to a quivering shell of need. His long fingers gently massaged the curves of her breasts, moving closer to her already tight nipples without actually touching them. Anticipation built inside her.

She squirmed closer, silently begging him to touch her there, but he was slow to respond. Closer and closer still until his thumbs lightly brushed over the tips of her nipples. One brief caress, then he was gone.

She groaned her frustration. Determined to tease him as much as he teased her, she withdrew from the kiss and began to suck on his lower lip. At the same time, she cupped his rear, digging her fingers into the firm flesh and bringing his arousal more closely in contact with her stomach. They both caught their breath.

"I want you," Nash breathed. "Naked."

His words increased her need, delighting her. In a smooth dance they'd performed before, they broke apart and quickly tugged at their clothes. She finished first and slid onto the cool sheet. Nash followed.

They lay facing each other, his leg between hers, his thigh pressing against her swollen dampness. As they kissed, he cupped her left breast. Their tongues stroked and played. When he retreated, she followed. His taste, his heat, his hardness all inflamed her. She could not be naked enough with this man. She wanted to be vulnerable, hungry and bare to him. Yes, she wanted the pleasure to follow, but for now it was enough to want him.

When he urged her onto her back, she went easily. He broke the kiss and knelt between her thighs. His mouth settled on her chest. As his tongue swept over and around the tight nipple, his fingers matched the action on her other breast. Her muscles tightened as pleasure poured through her, trickling down to increase her growing ache. She felt herself swelling, readying. Already she wanted him inside her, but that was for later. First Nash would want to make her beg.

He kept his attention on her breasts until she was close to breaking. Tension filled her body, making every muscle stiffen. When she nearly vibrated with need, he moved lower, placing openmouthed kisses on her belly, then lower still.

He reached for her hands and brought them to her center, where he had her part herself for him. She drew her knees back and dug her heels into the mattress. Her eyes were closed, but she knew he was close—she could feel his warm breath fanning her dampness. She was ready, so ready. Ready and aching. Her hips pulsed in silent invitation. And still he waited.

At last he moved close and pressed his tongue against her. Fire shot through her, making her jump and gasp. The single, slow lick was followed by another and another. Gentle, easy strokes that drove her to the edge of madness. He didn't go fast enough to take her to climax, but he didn't let the tension fall off, either.

She strained to get more pressure, she rocked her hips to get him to go faster. Neither worked. She tried begging.

''Nash, please.''

She felt the rumble of his laughter. In response to her plea, he inserted a finger inside her then curled it slightly, so it seemed to stroke her from the inside as his tongue did the same from the outside. He moved them in tandem. Slowly. Gently. Thoroughly. Bottom to top. Top to bottom. Over and over. Like the ticking of a clock. Ever so steady. Ever so slow.

Her entire body clenched. She couldn't breathe, couldn't think, couldn't do anything but focus on that incessant rhythm. Over and over. Tension grew and grew until she thought it would split her in two. More. She needed more. She needed—

He stopped completely. For the space of three heartbeats he hovered above her, not touching, not moving. Nothing. The wait was unbearable. Then he kissed her again, but more firmly this time, and faster.

She climaxed without warning. The release swept through her at the speed of sound, flinging her into paradise and making her cry out. Muscles contracted, her entire body spasmed in perfect pleasure. She was out of control and she never wanted that to change.

He continued to touch her, gentling the contact, until she had nothing left.

She opened her eyes and saw him smiling at her. She had to clear her throat before she could speak.

"That was more amazing than usual," she told him. "Which is saying something."

"You're easy to please."

"I'm glad you think so."

She lowered her gaze and saw that he was still hard. Her stomach clenched.

"I want you inside me," she said.

Words to live by, Nash thought as he reached for the condom he'd left on the nightstand. As he slipped it on, he studied the flush on Stephanie's chest and cheeks. The physical proof of her orgasm pleased him. He wanted her to enjoy their time in bed.

When he'd put on the protection, he slowly pushed into her. She was hot and wet. As he filled her, her muscles contracted around his erection, testing his control. He forced himself to hold back. He wanted her to come again.

Still kneeling, he shifted his weight off his arms so he could reach out to touch her breasts. They were always exquisitely sensitive after her first release. Just lightly brushing her nipples was usually enough to get her going again. He wanted to feel her rippling contractions and watch her face as she experienced wave after wave of orgasm. Her mouth would part slightly, her eyes would widen as she tried to keep looking at him. Sometimes he would swear he could see down to her soul.

Sure enough, with the first touch of his fingers, she gasped. He felt the tight clenching of her body. He thrust into her again and contractions massaged him. Blood surged into his arousal, pressure built in his groin, and still he held back.

Their gazes locked. With each rhythmic release, she sucked in a breath and whispered his name. Over and over, as if in prayer. He was getting closer, too, but he wanted this to go on as long as they both could stand it.

In and out, in and out. He got harder and harder. Deep inside everything collected for the surging release that was as inevitable as the tide. She continued to climax, massaging him, drawing him in deeper. Her breathing increased. He surged in faster and faster. They were both gasping.

At last he had to release her breasts and grasp her hips. He held onto her as he pumped in and out. She half raised off the bed. Her head dropped back as one massive contraction clenched around him...and he was lost.

His release exploded in a vortex of heat that

forced the air out of his body. He pushed in deeper, wanting her to take all of him. Her dampness continued to convulse around him, drawing out the bliss until there was nothing left for either of them but to fall together in a tangle of arms and legs.

Stephanie woke with a sense of contentment. She rolled onto her back and smiled. Last night had been amazing. More amazing than usual, which was saying something. But her feeling of happiness didn't just come from a night of great lovemaking. It also came from the recent changes in her life.

She liked Nash. Okay, she liked him a lot. She liked being around him and talking to him. She liked his parents and his brothers and their families. She liked the impact he'd made on her world. She liked how he was with her sons. Man, oh man, did she have it bad. Because liking him wasn't the problem.

She wanted more.

Stephanie sat up and tossed off the covers. "Don't be ridiculous," she said aloud. "There is no 'more' in this situation. You knew that when you started the affair."

But knowing and believing were two different things, at least in her world. She could list all the reasons it would never work—distance, her reluctance to trust a man to act like a partner and not a child, his emotional withdrawal from life since the death of his wife. Those were really big problems to get through. While they could be solved if both of them worked at it, so far she hadn't seen any indication that Nash wanted to change the status of things. Nor was she going to.

In a few days, when his vacation was over, he

would leave, and she would let him. No matter what, she wouldn't make a scene. It wasn't right to change the rules at this late date.

Not that she wanted to, she reminded herself. When Nash left, she would go on with her life and she would do just fine. Sure she would miss him, but she would get over it…wouldn't she?

Stephanie didn't want to think about any of that. She stretched and swung around to put her feet on the floor. As she did so she glanced at the clock. And actually screamed.

It was eight-thirty. In the morning. Her alarm had been set for six-thirty. What had happened?

Even as she fumbled for the switch and realized she'd forgotten to turn it on, adrenaline rushed through her body, galvanizing her into action. She raced into the bathroom where she quickly washed her face and brushed her teeth. A shower was going to have to wait. She had guests to feed.

In less than six minutes she was relatively groomed, dressed and racing down the stairs. The boys were already up—their doors were standing open—and she could hear voices from downstairs. Wincing at what Nash's parents must think of her, she jogged toward the kitchen and burst inside.

"Hey, Mom," Brett said from the table.

"Mommy!" the twins said together.

They were also at the table. They were eating breakfast. Pancakes and bacon from the looks of it. She stared around the room and saw Nash standing at the stove. The man was cooking!

"Morning," he said with a smile.

While it wasn't as unbelievable as having aliens land on her roof, it was darned close. Helping out was one thing, but cooking? Marty had always acted as if she were threatening to cut off his right arm if she ever suggested he prepare a meal himself.

She felt numb with shock. "I, ah, overslept," she said. "I forgot to set my alarm."

Nash's expression didn't change, but his eyes brightened with amusement. "You probably had other things on your mind."

That was true. She'd been so concerned about setting her travel clock so that she could get back to her own bed, that she'd forgotten about her regular alarm.

"My folks are in the dining room," he continued. "They have coffee, fruit and the newspaper. Howard wanted oatmeal which I've already fixed. Mom is raving about your scones and complaining about the weight she's going to put on. I have another batch in the oven."

He nodded at the stove. "I was fixing some eggs for myself. Do you want any?"

She'd slipped into an alternative universe. "Um, thanks."

"Okay. Oh, when I took the uncooked scones out of the freezer, I didn't know which to use, so I took a bag off the top shelf. I hope that's okay."

"It's fine."

"Brett told me what oven temperature to use."

She glanced at her oldest. "Thanks, honey."

He shrugged. "Nash said you were tired and we should let you sleep."

She could feel her cheeks getting hot. Nash was the reason she needed her rest.

"Coffee?" the man in question asked.

She nodded. He poured her a cup, then added milk and sugar, just the way she liked it.

Her throat was tight and her eyes burned. She had a bad feeling she was way too close to tears for comfort. Which made no sense. So he'd been nice— was that a reason to cry?

Sense or not, Nash's actions touched her in a way nothing had for years. Maybe ever. He'd taken care of her. Just like that, with no expectation of getting something back. She hadn't known that men like him existed. He made her feel she could count on him.

"You okay?" he asked.

She nodded again, knowing it was impossible to speak.

Just then she heard the sound of several cars pulling up.

"What's that?" Jason asked and got down from his seat. He ran toward the front of the house.

"They're all here," he called.

"Who?" Adam asked as he, too, left the kitchen. Brett was on his heels.

"Right on time," Nash said, glancing at the clock.

"On time for what?" she asked, her voice only a little scratchy.

Nash grinned. "You'll see."

Howard came through the swinging door. "Seems that the gang has all arrived. Ready to assign chores?"

"Sure."

Nash slid the scrambled eggs onto a plate, along with a couple of pieces of bacon. "Eat up," he said.

"You're going to need your strength. I'll be right back."

He walked out of the kitchen, heading toward the front door. Howard followed. Stephanie glanced from the plate to the door, and decided to see what was going on.

What she found stunned her nearly as much as seeing Nash cooking. Most of the Haynes clan had descended. All the brothers were there, along with Austin and several of the wives. There weren't as many children as usual. Instead of carrying food or drinks, this time everyone had gallons of paint, toolboxes, ladders and other building supplies. They gathered by the gatehouse, as if waiting for instructions. Nash stood in the center of the group.

As she approached, she saw that he held a list in his hand and was assigning tasks.

"Upstairs in the master, there's some ugly wallpaper in the bathroom. Did anyone bring the steamer?"

"Sure." Kyle patted the machine he'd set on the driveway. "I'll have that off by noon. Then we can put up the new paper."

"We'll do that," Elizabeth said as she put her arm around Hannah. "It's a floral pattern and we're going to care more about getting it right."

Travis groaned. "Any of us could do just as good a job."

"Sure you *could,* but do you want to?"

He kissed her. "Not on a bet."

Several people laughed. Stephanie felt as if her feet were nailed to the grass. She couldn't move, couldn't speak, couldn't protest what was happening. She watched as everyone trooped into her gate-

house and began to work. Nash finally noticed her
and walked over.

"You okay?" he asked.

"No. What are you doing?"

He stood facing her. "You'd ordered the paint
and wallpaper already," he said. "I didn't pick it
out."

"I know, but why are they here?"

"They're helping out because I asked. I know
you've been working on the gatehouse for a long
time. You want to move in there so you can get the
rest of the house renovated. I want to help. I'm leaving in a few days and I would like the gatehouse
done before I go. I guess I want to know that you're
going to be okay."

He spoke the last bit defiantly, as if he expected
her to be furious. She supposed she should be—he'd
been high-handed in arranging all this. But the truth
was, she was even closer to crying than before.

No one had ever wanted to take care of her before. No one had ever worried about her. They all
assumed she was so damn competent that she didn't
have doubts, didn't get tired, didn't sweat that it was
going to come out right.

She ached down to her bones. Not just because
he was being so sweet and nice and making her want
to beg him to never leave, but because what he was
doing was proof that he *was* leaving. If he'd considered changing his mind and staying, he wouldn't
want to have the gatehouse finished.

"You mad?" he asked.

She shook her head because she couldn't speak.

"Is it okay that I'm doing this?"

She managed a slightly strangled, "Yes."

"Will you be okay if I go help out?"

"Sure."

He touched her cheek, then walked toward the gatehouse.

Stephanie stood alone on her lawn and listened to the sound of people working and talking and laughing. She knew that she had to help out the others. It wasn't fair to leave everything to them. But first she had to get herself under control.

In that moment, when she'd realized what he was doing, something inside her had given way. It was as if some protective wall had crumbled to dust, leaving her exposed and vulnerable.

How could she help loving him? He wasn't even everything she'd ever wanted—he was more. A partner, a friend, a warm, caring lover who was as solid as a rock. He was her hero. A one-in-a-million kind of man.

A man who was leaving. And she didn't have a single right to ask him to stay.


By midafternoon, most of the rooms had been painted. Stephanie walked through the downstairs carrying cans of soda and bottles of water. The twins were circulating with granola bars and cookies.

The transformation of the dark old house into something bright and charming amazed her, as did everyone's friendliness. These people might be a part of Nash's family, but they made her feel welcome.

She handed Craig a bottle of water and started toward the kitchen. On the way she found Brett carefully sanding a baseboard in the hall.

"You're doing a great job," she said as she

stopped and crouched next to him. "That's pretty detailed work."

Her twelve-year-old looked up at her. His blue eyes were dark and troubled. "Nash got his whole family to help."

"I know. That was really nice of him, huh?"

Brett didn't answer. Instead he folded the sand-paper in half and twisted it in his hands. "He's still leaving, right?"

As much as Stephanie wished she could say otherwise, she had to agree. "Of course he is, honey. He has a life in Chicago, remember?"

"He's not so bad, you know?" Brett's voice sounded small. "He's not Dad, but that's okay."

Her stomach dove for her toes. When had her son let go of his resentment of Nash and why hadn't she seen it happening? She hadn't wanted any of her children to connect too closely with Nash because she hadn't wanted them hurt by his leaving.

"Brett, Nash is a really great guy. He's been fun to have around, but it was always temporary. You knew that."

She winced at her own words. Of course he knew. Reminding him wasn't going to make Nash's leaving easier.

"But he likes it here," Brett said, staring at the sandpaper rather than her. "I bet he'd want to move here if you asked him to."

"I know it seems like that to you. I agree that he's had a fun vacation, which is good. But he has a regular life waiting for him. He has a job and a home and friends." But not a woman. She knew he'd been alone since his wife's death. And yes, the sex was great, but was it enough to get him to relocate? She didn't think so.

"You could ask," Brett repeated.

"I could."

But she wouldn't. Not only did she not want to put Nash in the position of having to refuse her, she wasn't sure she would survive actually having to hear him say no.

By five the gatehouse was nearly finished. Nash walked from room to room, pleased with all that had been done. All that was left was the new carpeting. As soon as Stephanie had that installed, she and the boys could move in. They'd have their own place, away from the guests. She would be safe.

He could see her here—her furniture, the boys' books and toys. They would make the small house into a home.

Could he see himself here?

The question brought him up short. Did he want to be here? Did he want to stay with Stephanie and her sons? That would mean getting involved. Emotions weren't safe, he reminded himself. Emotions were messy and couldn't be controlled. If life was out of control—

His cell phone rang. He pulled it out of his shirt pocket and pushed Talk.

"Harmon here."

"It's Jack," his boss told him. "We have a situation."

Five minutes later Nash turned off the phone and jogged toward the main house. He found Stephanie in the kitchen with Brett. She took one look at his face and blanched.

"What's wrong?" she asked.

"My boss called. There's a hostage situation in San Francisco at a bank robbery gone bad. Shots have been fired. A helicopter's on its way to pick me up." He glanced at his watch. "It's coming from the army base and should be here in about six minutes."

He'd wondered how she would react to the crisis, but except for the loss of color in her face, she was in control. "Do you need me to get you anything? Most of your family has left. Your parents took the twins to the park. I'll tell them when they get back."

"I appreciate that. I don't know how long I'll be gone. These things can take time. Then there's paperwork afterwards."

She dismissed his comments with a wave of her hand. "Don't worry about that. I'll pack your things and you can call us and let me know where you want them sent."

Her assumption that he wouldn't be coming back surprised him. Yes, he only had a few days left of his vacation but—

"I'm glad you're leaving," Brett said fiercely.

Nash turned to the boy and saw him wipe the back of his hand across his eyes. Hell.

He knelt in front of Brett. "I'm sorry I have to go, but this is important."

"I don't care."

"I care very much. About my work and about you, your brothers and your mom."

"Then don't go."

The words shouldn't have mattered to him, but God help him, he liked hearing them.

"Some bad men are holding people hostage. I have to go. If I don't some of them might die."

"Then promise to come back."

Stephanie put her hands on Brett's thin shoulders. "Honey, don't. Remember what we talked about? Nash has his own life and it's not here."

They'd talked about him? He stood and tried to read her expression. "Stephanie…" He wasn't sure what to say.

She shook her head. "We both knew this was temporary, right? So it's ending sooner than we thought. At least we're saved from having a long, painful goodbye. It's like ripping off a bandage. Faster is better."

"Faster hurts more," he said.

"But it's over quicker."

He wanted to tell her he would come back. He wanted to tell her that he didn't want to go in the first place. But to what end?

Before he could figure out what words were right, he heard a familiar sound. "The helicopter's here."

Outside several sheriff's cars had blocked off the street. Nash saw Kyle talking to one of the helicopter pilots.

Nash bent down and hugged Brett. Then he straightened and pulled Stephanie close.

"Take care of yourself," she said as she stepped back. There were tears in her eyes.

He felt as if he'd been kicked in the gut. There were a thousand things to say and no time left. His heart heavy, his chest tight, he jogged to the helicopter. Kyle slapped him on the back as he climbed in.

"Don't get dead," he called.

Nash gave him a thumbs-up, then yelled at the pilot to take off. He watched out the window until Stephanie and Brett were no more than specks. When he couldn't see them anymore, he watched anyway, knowing they were still standing there.

## Chapter Fourteen

By five in the morning the San Francisco sky had turned pale gray. Nash had lost count of the cups of coffee he'd consumed. He'd managed to talk the bank robbers into releasing the bodies of the two men they'd killed before Nash had arrived, and one pregnant woman who had gone into early labor. There were still fifteen people and three men with guns inside the ground-floor bank building.

FBI agents, local police and SWAT teams circled the high-rise. There were sharpshooters in place. The media was being kept at bay, with a live news feed being set up across the street.

Jack sat with Nash in the specially equipped vehicle in front of the bank.

"Now what?" Jack asked.

Nash didn't have an answer. Becker, the guy he'd been talking to for the past several hours, had seemed like he was ready to discuss releasing more hostages, but then had hung up unexpectedly. The bank's surveillance cameras had been disconnected by Becker and his buddies when they'd first taken hostages, so getting a look inside that way wasn't an option. A long-range camera had shown the three men having what looked like a heated argument.

"I'm guessing one of them doesn't agree with Becker's plan to give up," Nash said.

Sometimes that happened. Some criminals would rather shoot it out and face death than accept the consequences of prison. If that was the case, if a man was prepared to die, there weren't many rescue options.

"Can we take any of them out?" Jack asked.

Nash looked down at the bank floor plan he'd been given. Becker had said the hostages were being held in the vault. The door was open, but the civilians were still out of the main section of the bank. If Becker was telling the truth, then the sharpshooters could fire into the bank without hitting the hostages.

"We can't take one of them out," Nash said. "Even if we planned an armed assault for one or two seconds later, there would still be enough time for hostages to be killed. What are the odds of us getting all three of them at once? I don't want any dead civilians. Not on my watch."

Jack nodded. In this situation, Nash was in charge.

Nash rose and stepped out onto the sidewalk. The street had been blocked off, which would be hell on the morning commute. His stomach grumbled.

Frowning, he tried to remember the last time he'd

eaten. Not since arriving. The men inside hadn't, either. Or the hostages. He picked up the specially equipped cell phone that not only connected with Becker, but also activated a recording device and transmitted the call back to the FBI truck.

As he punched in the number, he shifted slightly. Then he had to move again. What the hell?

A rumbling sound grew as the ground began to roll.

Nash swore. Great. Just what his morning needed. A damn earthquake.

The rolling grew in intensity, as did the roaring sound. People began to yell. A few screamed. He looked up at the tall buildings all around him and figured he'd better head for cover. Just then the doors of the bank burst open.

A tall, dark-haired man ran onto the sidewalk.

"Don't shoot," he yelled, holding a cell phone in one hand and a gun in the other. He tossed the gun on the ground.

Nash was on him in a second. "Becker?" he yelled, even as he twisted the man's arm behind him and physically dragged him away from the bank.

"That damn building is swaying like a boat," the man cried out. "It's gonna fall and I'm not going to be crushed to death like some bug."

Behind him, still in the bank, another man was screaming for Becker to get his sorry butt back inside. The ground continued to roll and shake, distracting everyone.

Nash grabbed his radio. "Now," he called out. "Get in there now!"

The rescue team swarmed the front of the bank. With the earthquake still rumbling Nash couldn't hear the crash of the bank's rear door being blown as the rest of the team entered that way. Three shots were fired, then there was silence. Nash clutched his radio.

"One gunman shot," a voice said. "One captured. The hostages are all safe."

"How are you going to explain the earthquake in your report?" Jack asked several hours later as he sat on a corner of Nash's temporary desk in the San Francisco office.

Nash leaned back in his chair. "Sometimes we get lucky. That's all it was."

"It was more than that," his boss said. "Before you arrived, they'd killed two people. You put a stop to that. You're good at what you do."

"Thanks."

Jack stood up. "Either I was wrong about you burning out or you got what you needed from your vacation. You're welcome to come back anytime you'd like." He grinned. "Is tomorrow too soon?"

Work. Nash's refuge. Was he ready to return so quickly?

"Let me get back to you on that," he said.

Jack raised his dark eyebrows. "You sure about that?"

Nash nodded. "I'll finish my report and see you on my way out."

"Fair enough."

He left and Nash turned his attention to the computer screen. But instead of entering his report, he found himself thinking about what had happened that morning. How a 4.2 earthquake had saved fifteen hostages. As he'd told Jack, it had been little more than dumb luck. As always, there were circumstances out of everyone's control. Even his.

He placed his fingers on the keyboard, then dropped his hands back onto the desk. Well, hell. What do you know, he thought grimly. He couldn't control the world. If he were honest with himself, he might admit he couldn't control much of anything. Life happened, and he didn't get to decide which way it was going to go. He'd never been able to decide. No matter what he wanted or expected or needed, life had its own plan and didn't consult with him.

Today he'd gotten lucky. Two years ago, he hadn't.

Nash rose and crossed to the window. He stared out at the skyline of the city, but instead of seeing the tall buildings, he saw the bomb explosion that had killed his wife.

He hadn't known. No one had known. Tina had acted impulsively. He hadn't killed her. He'd never been responsible. Maybe he'd never believed he was. Maybe wallowing in guilt over not stopping her death had been easier than facing the truth—he felt guilty because he'd never loved her.

He should never have married her. He saw that now. Maybe he'd always known that, too. But he'd been in his late twenties. It had been time for him to get married, settle down. She'd been there and she'd wanted him. He'd been flattered. When she'd suggested making things permanent, he couldn't think of a reason to say no. He cared about her, they got along. He hadn't known what love felt like. He hadn't known the possibilities.

But after a few months, he'd seen that they'd

made a mistake. He'd tried to talk to Tina, but she'd refused to admit there was anything wrong. After a night of fighting, they'd gone to work and she'd been killed.

She'd deserved to be loved. Everyone did.

Including him.

Nash stiffened. Had he been the only one living out a part, or had Tina, too, been going through the motions? He would never know. He couldn't go back and make things right with her. But he could make the future better. He could let go of what had happened. He could learn from his mistakes. He could risk living again. He could risk love and belonging or he could continue to live on the outside, always looking in, never connecting.

One way was safe, one was guaranteed to be complicated and messy. What did he want? And what was he willing to risk to get it?

The twins sat on the edge of the bed and watched while she packed up Nash's clothes. According to the news, the hostage situation had ended that morning. Stephanie had been half expecting to get a phone call, but when noon came and went without a word, she accepted the fact that he was gone forever.

Reminding herself that she'd been the one to say he didn't have to come back wasn't making her feel any better. Nor were the boys' long faces.

Jason swung his feet back and forth, clunking his heels against the pedestal of the sleigh bed. "But Nash likes being here," he said mournfully.

"I know he had a good time," she said as she

folded shirts and stacked them together. "You're supposed to enjoy your vacation."

Adam didn't speak. Instead he stared at her with eyes full of hurt.

Her own control was already more than a little shaky. It wouldn't take much to push her over the edge. She tried to smile.

"We'll be fine," she told the boys. "It's summer, so there's no school. Isn't that a good thing?"

They both nodded without a lot of enthusiasm. She knew how they felt. In less than a week, the B&B would be filled. She would be running around like a crazy person. But the thought of paying guests and plenty of work didn't ease the sharp pain in her chest. She felt as if her entire world had been shattered.

No more relationships, she vowed silently. She and the boys couldn't handle it. She'd gone and fallen in love with the first guy she'd slept with since Marty's death. Her sons were missing Nash, as well. If one man could mess up her life in just a couple of weeks, what would happen if she actually risked dating?

It wouldn't be the same, a small voice whispered. She sighed, knowing the words were true. She'd fallen in love with Nash. It didn't matter who she dated. He'd claimed her heart and it would be a long time before she was able to offer it to someone else again.

She dropped the shirts into the open suitcase, then faced the twins.

"I can't believe it's barely the first week of summer and you two have long faces," she said.

"Brett says he's not coming out of his room," Jason told her.

"I know. But you know what? I have a great idea that's going to make us all feel better."

Neither twin looked convinced. She didn't feel convinced, either, but she was going to pretend to be fine—for their sake. Tonight, like last night, she would lie awake, missing Nash, longing for him, wishing it could have been different. But during the day, she would keep it all together.

"We're going to the pool," she said and waited for the cheers.

"Okay," Jason muttered.

Adam simply slid off the bed and walked out of the room.

Stephanie stepped into the hall and crossed to the bottom of the stairs. "Brett, get your swimsuit," she yelled. "We're going to the pool. And yes, you have to go."

Vivian opened her door. "Is everything all right?" she asked kindly. "The boys seem very quiet today."

"They're missing Nash," Stephanie admitted. "I thought hanging out at the pool with their friends would help."

Vivian's dark eyes turned knowing. "Will it help you?"

"I'm a little old to be healed by water sports," she said, determined to keep her tone light. "But it's always fun to get out."

She waited for Vivian to ask more questions, but Nash's mother simply smiled. "Do you mind if Howard and I tag along? We're enjoying our time with the boys."

Stephanie hesitated. The last thing she needed was for her sons to bond with more people who were leaving. But it would be rude to say no. Besides, on a purely selfish level, she liked hanging around with Nash's folks. Not only did they remind her a little of him, they were good people whose company she enjoyed.

"You're more than welcome," she said. "Just be warned that it gets pretty noisy."

"No problem. Give us five minutes to get ready."

The Glenwood community pool complex was as crowded and loud as Stephanie had imagined it would be. There were actually three pools—a shallow one for children under the age of six, a six-lane lap pool and a massive round pool that dated back to the fifties when a rich newspaper baron had moved to town and donated the land and money for the structure. Over the years, the main pool had been refurbished, but the original shape had never been changed.

Stephanie led her group to a place in the shade. Most of the older kids and teenagers congregated on the cement border of the pool, while the families took up residence on the grassy slope leading to the video-game hut and snack bar. She spread out towels, double-checked that the boys had been covered in sun block, then gave them the okay to head for the water.

She promised Vivian and Howard that she would return shortly, then made her way to one of the half-dozen lifeguards on duty. There she gave the names and ages of her three boys, pointed them out and confirmed they had each attended swimming classes and were strong swimmers.

She was about to return to Nash's parents when someone tapped her on the shoulder. She turned and saw Elizabeth Haynes.

"I didn't know you were coming to the pool today," she said with a smile. "There's a group of us here." Elizabeth laughed. "I suppose we always travel in groups, don't we? Have you heard from Nash?"

As several of the Haynes brothers had still been around when Nash had left, word of his assignment had spread quickly. That morning she'd received a couple of calls asking for updates. She wasn't sure why anyone in his family thought he would stay in touch and the reminder that he hadn't didn't make her feel any better. Still, they were nice people who weren't responsible for her broken heart and she did her best to be polite.

"I saw on the news that the hostage situation ended successfully," she said. "But other than that I don't know anything."

Elizabeth smiled. "I'm sure he'll be back shortly."

Stephanie nodded, even though she doubted she would ever see him again. Oh, they might run into each other sometime when he was out visiting family or here for the war games, but by the time that happened she intended to be well over him. Which meant she shouldn't plan on crossing paths with him for about twenty-five years.

"Are Kevin and Haley with you?" Stephanie asked. "Vivian and Howard have braved the pool."

She pointed up to where they'd placed their towels. Elizabeth glanced toward them and waved.

"Let me go tell the others," she said. "We'll join you."

Stephanie couldn't protest—not without sounding rude. And it wasn't that she didn't like the Haynes family—it was just that they reminded her too much of Nash.

It was only for one afternoon, she told herself as she returned to Vivian and Howard and prepared for the onslaught. She could survive that. Tonight, when she was alone, she would give in to the tears that hovered right beneath the surface of her self-control. Eventually the raw edge of the pain would dull into something bearable.

In a matter of minutes Elizabeth and company had joined them. Names of children in the pool were passed around and Haley and Elizabeth took the first shift of watch. Stephanie sat next to Rebecca who made her laugh with tales of teaching her oldest son, David, the ins and outs of using the washing machine.

"He didn't believe me about sorting colors," Rebecca told her. "And there was this bright red T-shirt."

"I know exactly what happened."

Rebecca grinned. "The boy has pink underwear. He's humiliated."

Stephanie tried to concentrate on the conversation. But Kevin was with them, as was Kyle, and every time she caught sight of a tall, dark-haired man, she thought of Nash. Her heart instantly started pounding and her thighs went up in flames. Then she had to remind herself that he was gone. When that happened, a fresh wave of pain swept through her and threatened to pull her under.

She found herself wishing for the impossible and imagining what life would have been like if Nash had wanted to stay. If he'd fallen in love with her, the way she'd fallen for him.

Rebecca leaned close. "Whatever happens, I want you to know the family will always be there for you."

"I appreciate that," Stephanie told her.

She knew what Rebecca meant—that even if things didn't work out for her and Nash, the family would still look out for her. She could call on them in a time of need. Another kindness, she thought, trying to be grateful. There was no way for Rebecca to know the words sounded like the closing of a metal door, locking her in a prison of memories from which she would never escape.

The twins climbed out of the pool and ran up the slope. She picked up their towels and handed them over as the boys approached.

"How's the water?" she asked.

"Not too cold," Jason told her.

Adam frowned slightly. "Brett's talking to a girl," he said, the confusion in his voice making it clear he didn't understand why anyone sensible would want to do that.

"Really?"

At twelve? Was that the right age for that sort of thing to start? She glanced around the pool and found her son sitting on the edge on the far side. Next to him was a pretty red-haired girl with a bright smile. Brett said something, then ducked his head. The girl laughed.

Stephanie's longing for Nash increased. She wanted him to be here to share the moment. She wanted to ask him how things were going to be different as her son became a teenager. She wanted—

"Are you all right?" Rebecca asked in a low voice.

Stephanie nodded, then had to brush unexpected tears from her cheeks. She couldn't speak. Not without breaking into sobs. Control, she told herself. She had to get control.

Rebecca said something else, but Stephanie couldn't hear her. It took her a second to figure out that a loud noise had filled the sky. She looked up and saw a helicopter approaching.

"It's Nash," Jason yelled as he scrambled to his feet.

Stephanie couldn't blame her son—that was her first thought, too. Even so, she told both him and herself it wasn't possible.

"Nash wouldn't take a helicopter back to Glenwood," she said. Assuming he was even coming back.

But Jason didn't care. He raced toward the rear fence of the complex and swung open the gate. Adam was on his heels. As she got to her feet, Brett ran past her.

"It's Nash," he called. "Hurry!"

She walked after them. Even if it *was* Nash, his return didn't mean anything had changed. She was going to have to talk with the boys tonight and remind them that Nash had been a guest and nothing more. They weren't—

She froze just inside the gate. Once again two sheriff's cars blocked off the street as the helicopter set down. Her heart pounded painfully in her chest as a tall, dark-haired man stepped out.

Her sons flung themselves at Nash. She couldn't hear what they were saying, but Nash bent low and hugged them all. Her eyes filled with more tears. She couldn't do this, she thought. She couldn't pretend she didn't care, which meant she was about to make a fool out of herself in a very public way.

But even the threat of humiliation didn't stop her from running toward him.

Nash straightened and held out his arms. She crashed into him and hung on, knowing she never wanted to let go. She wanted to be with this man forever. Did she have the courage to tell him the truth? Did she really think she could hide it?

"I missed you," he whispered, wrapping his arms around her so tightly she could barely breathe. "Every minute."

The intensity of his words gave her hope.

"Me, too."

He kissed her hard, then pulled back enough to look at her face. His dark eyes blazed with a fire she'd never seen before. "I want to change the rules," he said. "I don't want to be a temporary guest. I don't want to leave. I want to make things complicated and messy and permanent. I love you, Stephanie. I love you in ways I've never loved anyone before. I want to marry you and grow old with you. I want us to have one of those marriages that makes young couples sigh with envy. I want to have a baby with you. If the legend is true, you'll even get that girl you want."

She couldn't speak, couldn't think, couldn't do

anything but listen to the melodic sound of his perfect words. He loved her? Really?

"You love me?"

"Yeah. Are you shocked?"

Relief and happiness and promise and hope swept through her making her feel as if she could float on air.

"I'm stunned," she said, then kissed him. "I love you, too. I know I wasn't supposed to, but I couldn't help myself."

"I'm not about to complain. Will you marry me, Stephanie? I know we have a lot of details to work out, but they're just logistics. I can relocate. Hell, I can get a different job. I just want to be with you and the boys."

Someone tugged on her T-shirt. She looked down and saw her kids standing next to them.

"Say yes, Mom," Brett told her.

Nash chuckled. "Okay, guys, we need a little privacy."

The boys grumbled, but took a few steps back. He turned back to her.

"I know the last time you ran off with someone you'd only known a few weeks, it was a disaster. So if you want to take things slow, I'll understand. I want to be a partner in this marriage. I want us to take care of each other. It's not going to be one-sided, but I'm willing to prove that to you, rather than have you take my word."

"Oh, Nash." She leaned against him and sighed. "You've already proved that a hundred times over. I love you and I want to be with you always." She looked into his eyes. "Yes, I'll marry you. There's nothing I want more."

"All right." Nash pulled her off her feet and swung her around. "She said yes," he yelled.

There was a collective cheer. For the first time she noticed the Haynes/Harmon/Reynolds clan had gathered around them.

"We have an audience," she murmured.

"I know. They're my family. Your family, now. Maybe we should give them a show."

He lowered her back to the ground and pressed his mouth to hers. It was a kiss of love, of passion and promise. Stephanie responded in kind, as words of congratulations washed over them.

*My family,* Nash had said with pride. He was no longer the man on the outside, looking in, she thought happily. He'd become a part of them, and of her. He'd come home.

\* \* \* \* \*

*If you enjoyed ONE IN A MILLION,*
*you will love the next book*
*in Susan Mallery's*

HOMETOWN HEARTBREAKERS

*series:*
*QUINN'S WOMAN*
*Available August 2003*
*Don't miss it!*

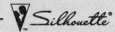

If you enjoyed what you just read,
then we've got an offer you can't resist!

# Take 2 bestselling
# love stories FREE!
# Plus get a FREE surprise gift!

**Clip this page and mail it to Silhouette Reader Service™**

**IN U.S.A.**
3010 Walden Ave.
P.O. Box 1867
Buffalo, N.Y. 14240-1867

**IN CANADA**
P.O. Box 609
Fort Erie, Ontario
L2A 5X3

**YES!** Please send me 2 free Silhouette Special Edition® novels and my free surprise gift. After receiving them, if I don't wish to receive anymore, I can return the shipping statement marked cancel. If I don't cancel, I will receive 6 brand-new novels every month, before they're available in stores! In the U.S.A., bill me at the bargain price of $3.99 plus 25¢ shipping and handling per book and applicable sales tax, if any*. In Canada, bill me at the bargain price of $4.74 plus 25¢ shipping and handling per book and applicable taxes**. That's the complete price and a savings of at least 10% off the cover prices—what a great deal! I understand that accepting the 2 free books and gift places me under no obligation ever to buy any books. I can always return a shipment and cancel at any time. Even if I never buy another book from Silhouette, the 2 free books and gift are mine to keep forever.

235 SDN DNUR
335 SDN DNUS

| Name | (PLEASE PRINT) | |
| --- | --- | --- |
| Address | Apt.# | |
| City | State/Prov. | Zip/Postal Code |

\* Terms and prices subject to change without notice. Sales tax applicable in N.Y.
\*\* Canadian residents will be charged applicable provincial taxes and GST.
   All orders subject to approval. Offer limited to one per household and not valid to
   current Silhouette Special Edition® subscribers.
   ® are registered trademarks of Harlequin Books S.A., used under license.

SPED02                                    ©1998 Harlequin Enterprises Limited

# Have you ever wanted to be part of a romance reading group?

Be part of the Readers' Ring, Silhouette Special Edition's exciting book club!

Don't miss the next title!

## BALANCING ACT

by Lilian Darcy
(SE #1552)

Available July 2003

Encourage your friends to engage in lively discussions by using the suggested reading group questions provided at the end of the novel. Also, visit the **www.readersring.com** Web site for engaging interactive materials related to this novel.

*Available at your favorite retail outlet.*

*Silhouette®*

*Where love comes alive™*

# COMING NEXT MONTH

**SPECIAL EDITION**